RUINED

A DECADENCE AFTER DARK EPILOGUE

M. NEVER

RUINED
Copyright © M. NEVER 2015
All rights reserved

Cover Design By:
Marisa Shor, Cover Me, Darling

Editing By:
Jenny Carlsrud Sims, Editing 4 Indies

Copy Editing By:
Candice Royer

Proofreading By:
Nichole Strauss, Perfectly Publishable

Interior Design and Formatting By:
Christine Borgford, Perfectly Publishable

DEDICATION

For the readers . . .

PROLOGUE

KAYNE

C.S. LEWIS ONCE SAID, "LIFE is too deep for words, so don't try to describe it, just live it."

ELLIE

"ELLIE! BREAKFAST!" KAYNE'S VOICE BOOMS through the house. "You can come down now, kitten!"

I stretch atop the cluster of pillows laid out for me on the floor. Kayne and I have been playing, and I've been bad—*again*. I smile to myself as my muscles elongate. I like being bad.

"Ellie!" he calls again.

All right, I'm coming. Hopefully, several times this morning. I pull myself up onto my hands and knees and stretch once more, like the lazy, spoiled kitten I am. The bushy white tail inserted in my behind shifts, sending a frizzle of pleasure up my spine. I take a quick glance around the brightly lit room; the sunlight is pouring through every window, highlighting the abundance of metal as I crawl past it. Similar to my living quarters in Mansion, Kayne and I have converted the sitting room off our bedroom into our own personal play space. Three hundred square feet decorated with crops and whips on the wall, a bondage horse, a swing suspended from the ceiling, a leather chest full of sex toys, and one table of torture. Oh, and my bed made up of fluffy white pillows on the floor. He loves watching me sit there, sleep there, beg there. I won't lie; I love it, too.

I crawl out of the bedroom and down the stairs of our magnificent home, migrating toward the kitchen. Sometimes I still can't believe it's ours. I never imagined I'd live somewhere so beautiful, spacious, and warm. Truth be told, I never imagined I'd be involved in a BDSM marriage where I crawled around on the floor half the time either. But hey, c'est la vie, right?

The tag on my collar jingles as I reach the first floor and make my way to where Kayne is standing by the stove. I may be the one on my hands and knees, but he's the one doing the cooking. Don't be fooled, I'm not the only one who's trained. I kneel right beside him.

"'Bout time, kitten." He pets my head and continues to cook. It smells like pancakes, but I can't be sure. It might be waffles. I can't exactly see from my vantage point on the floor.

"Did you think about what a bad little kitten you are?" he asks without looking at me.

"Maybe," I answer.

"Maybe?" He glances down with a raised eyebrow.

"I thought about how maybe I like being bad," I inform him.

"There's no 'maybe' about it." He chuckles, shirtless and completely drool worthy. Cut abs, defined chest, and chiseled arms. A barbed wire tattoo circling one flexing bicep, writing scribbled across his rib cage, and my personal favorite, a colorful compass with my name on it over his heart. If I were wearing panties, they'd be drenched.

"Go outside. I'll be there in a minute," he orders, grabbing a plate from the cabinet.

I sit for a second, not obeying immediately as he expects. I'm going to get in so much trouble.

"Is there a problem, kitten?" Kayne asks with a hint of menace. I may not call him Master but, for all intents and purposes, he is. And 'Master' does not like it when I'm disobedient. I, however, love to push his buttons.

"No, Kayne," I drawl, still kneeling beside him.

"Then get." His blue eyes flash and my stomach muscles clench.

"Yes, Kayne." I place my hands on the cool tile floor and begin to crawl out of the kitchen and into the living room where the doors to the lanai are wide open. There's a breeze coming off the ocean and the sky is a deep cobalt blue. I have never once regretted moving to paradise. Even after . . . well, I don't want to ruin the mood by thinking about that.

I kneel on the pillow next to the table. Most mornings, I sit in a chair like a civilized human being, but today, we're playing. And it's so much fun when we play. I, however, always wear neck jewelry, whether it's my inconspicuous slave collar or my real one. This morning, I woke up with Kayne's head between my legs and the thick white leather one around my throat. He had that look in his eyes—the starving beast wanted to feed.

I notice the table already has cut fruit, orange juice, and one place setting right before Kayne appears with a plate of pancakes and a bottle of syrup. I can almost guarantee this is going to get messy. He loves to get me dirty and then clean me up— *with his tongue.* I shiver internally at just the thought.

Kayne places the plate and syrup down then sits in the chair directly in front of me. He's angled it so he can access both the table and me.

"Closer." He yanks on my collar wedging me between his legs. "Much better." He slides his hand down my chest and massages one of my breasts. I close my eyes and inhale as sensations start to brew from the rough way he kneads and pulls on my nipple. We haven't had sex in over a week, and I am seriously frustrated. I'm fairly certain he's been planning this little escapade.

My frustration is a large part of the reason I got into trouble. I touched when I wasn't supposed to. (More like put my mouth where I wasn't supposed to.)

"Are you going to behave while I feed you?" he asks as he pulls away and begins to put food on his plate. Some fresh mango, a pancake, and a drizzle of syrup.

"I can't make any promises," I purr.

He pauses as he cuts the pancake. "You know the more you misbehave the more severe the punishment?"

"I know." *This isn't my first rodeo.*

"But you're willing to push me anyway?" He picks up a small triangle from his plate and feeds it to me.

I nod as I chew, my heated gaze mirroring his.

"You made me come when you weren't supposed to." He feeds me another piece of pancake. I take it from his hand, sucking the syrup off his fingers as seductively as I can.

"I know." I watch as he picks up a piece of mango and places it in front of me. I open my mouth, but he pulls it back. Shaking his head, he rings the orange-colored fruit around my lips like he's applying lip gloss.

4

"Lick," he orders me. I run my tongue over the sweet juice coating my lips. "I wanted to take this slow. I wanted to savor you in the fresh air. Build you up and break you down until you were begging . . ."

"I'll still beg," I hastily interrupt him.

"You just love being naughty." He grabs my chin. "I never gave you permission to speak."

I smile wickedly. "I don't need your permission to speak."

"Oh, no? What do you need permission for?"

"To come."

"And is that what you want?"

"Yes."

"Naughty kittens don't get to come." His voice vibrates with authority.

"Yes, they do," I argue with him.

"Not by my hand."

"I have my own hands."

"You're not supposed to touch yourself unless I say so."

"You said it yourself . . . I'm naughty."

"Yes, you are." He leans in and kisses me, a ravishing assault that warns me about what's to come. By the time Kayne pulls away, my lips are throbbing and so is my clit. I need him to touch me, sate me, but I know that's not in the plans for a very long while.

Breathing heavily, he hauls me off the floor and lays me out on the tabletop.

"Open," he orders, lifting my legs so my ass is hanging just off the edge of the table. My thighs are wide, and I'm on display. I know I'm glistening in the sunlight; I've never been good at controlling my arousal, especially when my husband's tongue is mere inches away from me.

"Kayne," I whimper, wanting to clench my thighs as my pussy tingles.

"Yes?" He hovers over my slit as close as humanly possible but never touches it. The only thing I can feel is the warm caress of his breath mingled with the morning breeze.

"You want my tongue on you?" he asks, a hair away from my wide-open folds.

"Yes," I rasp.

"Yes, what?"

"Yes, please." I twitch.

"I don't think that's the right answer."

"Yes, Kayne," I correct myself. My excitement is getting the better of me as he strokes my tail, teasing me with the plug lodged deeply in my ass.

Kayne drapes my legs over his shoulders then reaches for the syrup. *I knew this was going to get messy.*

"You had your breakfast. Now, it's time for mine." He squeezes the bottle and coats my pussy with the sticky substance. It's lukewarm and tickles as it drips down my heated pink flesh. "Come and I'll spank you."

"Promise?" I ask just as he puts his mouth on me and begins to lick. My muscles immediately spasm.

"Oh, shit!" I cry out as he laps up every last drop of syrup while simultaneously fucking me with the plug. My tiny little rosebud expands and contracts as Kayne mercilessly eats me alive. I know I shouldn't come, but his threat is just too enticing. I want it rough. I want him to punish me. I want him to fuck me so hard that we're both launched far, far away.

"Kayne!" I scream as I let go, pulling his hair as my orgasm cripples me. He licks harder and pumps the plug faster until he squeezes out every possible drop of my arousal. *Oh god, I needed that. Desperately.* He then lifts his head and looks up at me over my heaving chest, his eyes a sharp, piercing blue in the sunlight, the brown patch bold and dominant. Just like my 'Master.'

"You are a very bad little girl," he says as he shifts, pulling me down the table and placing me on my feet.

"I know," I respond with satisfaction.

"How many lessons do I have to teach you before one sticks?"

"Many. I'm a slow study."

"I've noticed. Clean up breakfast then come upstairs," he orders resolutely.

"Yes, Kayne," I answer obediently.

With that he steps away — his erection standing tall and proud — and disappears inside. I know I'm in trouble. A delicious kind of earth-shattering trouble that's going to both push my limits and send me soaring.

I clean up quickly, placing the dishes in the sink and covering the fruit and pancakes; I know Kayne will house them later. The man eats like he's a growing teenage boy.

I hurry up the stairs and into our bedroom. It's cleanly decorated in creams and whites with bold pops of color. It has a tranquil, airy feel, like an island escape.

I drop to all fours before I enter the playroom. Kayne is already waiting for me, leaning up against the bondage horse wielding his weapon of choice—a riding crop.

He hits it against the palm of his hand, watching me intently as I crawl across the room and kneel right at his feet.

"So here we are," he states. "Is this what you wanted, kitten?" He uses the end of the crop to lift my face.

"Yes," I squeak, then clear my throat and answer again more confidently. "Yes."

"Kitten, kitten, kitten. You love to be punished as much as I love to punish you. What a pair we make."

I smile up at him. "Is there anything wrong with being made for each other?"

"No, baby. Not a damn thing." He holds my face in place.

"What's your safe word, Ellie?"

"Cupcake."

Kayne nods. We go through this ritual every time. In the four years we've been married, I have never used my safe word, no matter how far he's pushed me. And there were times it was pretty far. But every experience has brought us closer together. I don't think today will be any different.

"On." He smacks the horse with the crop and the crack echoes throughout the room.

What makes Kayne so skilled at enlivening my emotions is the element of surprise. I never know what he's going to do or what direction he's going to turn. We don't use the horse very often. Truth be told, I don't get punished a whole lot. The last time was a few months ago. We've shifted more toward kinky sex than anything else, but every so often, our beasts demand to be let out.

I climb onto the black padded contraption with restraints on all four legs. Straddling it, I rest on my stomach as Kayne fastens my wrists first and then my ankles. The cuffs are tight and barely leave any wiggle room. He did that on purpose. In this position, my ass and back are completely vulnerable. The leather is cool against my cheek, but my skin is on fire. My breathing quickens.

"Comfortable, kitten?" Kayne runs the crop over my bare back. "Or are you beginning to regret ever being bad?"

I always have a little bit of anxiety when I'm strapped down about to be punished. It's what makes this experience so illicit. "No. I don't regret it," I force out.

He leans over and rasps in my ear, "Such a brave little kitten even when she's scared." I shake with anticipation, excitement, and a small amount of fear. Then I hear the crop cut through the air and connect on my ass cheek. "Kayne!" I jump, but the ankle and wrist cuffs restrain me; I'm not budging an inch.

"You wanted this, kitten," he reminds me as he lands another blow.

"Ouch!" My behind stings.

Kayne rubs the inflamed skin until it tempers. He doesn't utter a sound, knowing the silence is killer. Then, without warning, he whacks me on the opposite cheek. My body tenses all over again, my muscles gripping at the butt plug while my clit rubs against the unforgiving leather.

"Those were just warm-up shots." Kayne walks around the horse until he's standing in front of me. His blinding erection right in my face.

"Pick your head up. Open your mouth," he directs. I do as he says; my head the only part of my body I can move. As I open my mouth, he pulls his shorts down, springing himself free. He then grabs the back of my head, gripping a handful of hair, and slides his cock in until it feels like it's touching my tonsils. "Good girl. Now swallow me." He pumps shallowly, keeping eighty percent of his erect length in my mouth. I fight to keep my jaw open and not choke on my spit as he pummels me. My eyes start to water and I pull against the restraints as he purposely gags me. He was never going to spank me. This was always going to be my punishment. I went down on him this morning when he told me not to, and he ended up coming rampantly in my mouth. Then I added fuel to the fire at the table outside by deliberately disobeying him.

He buries his cock all the way down my throat and we both

have our own reaction. He shivers with lust, and I whimper helplessly. He then pulls out spontaneously, breathing erratically. "Going to think twice before putting your mouth where it's not allowed?"

I sputter then grin deviously. "Maybe," I pant.

"Maybe, your ass," he mocks, repositioning himself behind me and landing another blow with the crop. *Oh, shit.*

The kinetic energy in the room electrifies as I feel Kayne move about. I hear one of the drawers to the chest open and close before I feel the warmth of his body behind me once again. A second later, the distinct sound of the lubrication top pops.

"I'm going to fuck you hard, Ellie." The distance is blatant in his voice, the overpowering arousal taking over, making him blind with need.

"Kayne." My response is timid, hesitant.

"You asked for this, kitten."

He's right, I did. I want it. Doesn't mean I'm not scared.

I hear his inconsistent breaths as he inserts one finger into my entrance.

"Get wet for me, baby." He pumps his hand fast then adds a second finger and then a third. Before I know it, I'm grinding my clit against the hard leather, sprinting after an orgasm I didn't even see coming.

"Keep rubbing, kitten." Kayne continues to finger me as he yanks the tail from my ass. My body locks up because I know what's coming. He spanks me, and I let out a shrill cry. He hits me again and again, with all three fingers buried inside me. I don't know which is torturing me more, the pleasure or the sting of pain. I reach the precipice fast and hard.

"Kayne, please may I come?!" I wail, my pussy clenching and my clit aching.

"Come, kitten. Come." There's turmoil in his voice. Just as I let go and begin to freefall, Kayne withdraws his fingers and smears my arousal up into my pulsating buttonhole. He then plunges every inch of his concrete cock into my ass at once. I yelp like a wounded dog as his erection and my orgasm tear me right in two. The pain as shocking as the pleasure.

I cling to the wave of my climax for as long as possible while Kayne fucks me with reckless abandonment until he reaches his own peak.

"Fuck, I'm going to come." He grunts, pulling on my hair. "Baby, you feel so good, you're going to make me come." He slams into me and I jerk forward in the restraints, my ankles and wrists straining, the tears flowing freely.

"Kayne!"

With one more deafening blow, he unleashes, coming deep inside my exploited ass and limp body.

In the aftermath, there's nothing but static, sunlight, and the sound of our tattered breathing in the now stormless room.

"Hey." Kayne kisses me softly, licking up the tears that are still flowing steadily down my cheeks.

"Hey." I sniffle, looking up at him in my peripheral vision.

"You okay?"

"Yeah." I smile, and I am.

"I love you," he whispers, still licking and kissing my face.

"I know." I close my eyes serenely. "And no one loves you more than I do."

"Only by the grace of God."

He's trying to be funny, but Kayne's funny always has a bit of truth behind it. In this case, anyway. He still feels like he doesn't deserve me, and I came to terms a long time ago that it's just a character flaw we both have to live with. Doesn't mean I won't keep trying to drill it into his head that he is loved and more deserving than he believes.

Kayne kisses me one last time before he withdraws himself from my body. My taut little butthole relaxes for the first time today. I breathe more easily as all the tension uncurls itself from my limbs.

"Hang tight, kitten. I'll clean you up." *Like I have any other option.* Kayne returns from the bathroom with a damp washcloth and caringly wipes away the sticky remnants before he unfastens each restraint; rubbing my wrists and ankles as he goes. When I'm finally free, he urges me to sit up then lifts me into his arms.

Lethargically, I mold myself to him, resting my head on his chest. He tightens his hold, keeping me close.

I'm nearly asleep by the time he places me in bed and curls up beside me.

I snuggle up next to him, placing my ear over his heart, letting the strong, steady sound soothe me like it always does.

"Did I hurt you, Ellie?" he asks with a hint of worry as he runs one finger through my hair.

"You utterly ruined me." That's always my response after a bout of rough sex. It's my way of telling him no one will ever compare to the way he loves me, physically or emotionally.

"Good." There's contentment in his voice. "You're such a naughty little kitten."

"I know. You made me that way." I look up at him.

"I know. Do you hate me for it?"

"Does it seem like I hate you?"

"No."

"Then there's your answer."

Kayne hugs me tighter as I stare up at him, and then glance away immediately once our eyes meet.

I feel his energy shift. "Ask me, Ellie."

Shit. Kayne has told me repeatedly that I can't hide anything from him, and as hard as I try to conceal what I'm thinking, one evasive glance always gives me away.

I nibble on my lip, hesitant to go down this road.

"Ellie . . ." Kayne nudges me, urging me to talk. He gets agitated when he knows that I'm deliberately keeping something from him. I chew on my lip harder.

"I want to be more naughty," I state timidly.

"More naughty?" His eyebrows shoot up.

I nod cautiously, knowing this conversation could be world war three in the making. "I want to know what it's like to be with two men."

There, I said it, and should now probably take cover.

The severity of Kayne's silence tells me everything I need to know. I just pissed him off big time. It doesn't happen often, but when it does, it's frightening. I think I just pierced my tongue with my incisor. I never should have said a damn thing.

Kayne suddenly expels a heated breath. "Do you really want to be with Jett that badly?"

"I really want to be with both of you that badly," I clarify. "It isn't just about Jett."

He stares up at the ceiling. I know he's at war with himself.

He wants to give me what I want without losing himself in the process. The last time Jett, London, Kayne, and I fooled around, we took it further than we ever have before. For the first time, I was sexually intimate with Jett. I don't even know how it happened, natural progression maybe, but my lips ended up around his dick. I sucked him off, while Kayne fucked me from behind, and London sat on his face. That was only a few weeks ago, but I haven't stopped thinking about it since. Haven't stopped thinking about Jett and Kayne sandwiching me together and taking me at the same time.

"I know you didn't hate watching me with him. You fucked me the exact same way you do when I'm with London."

"How's that?" he questions.

"Recklessly."

His lips twitch. "It wasn't so bad watching you suck another man's dick."

"You liked it?"

Kayne maintains his silence.

"Did you like having threesomes with Jett?"

"I like threesomes, period. But I always used to lean toward me being the minority. Jett used to like sharing his woman. Engulfing their senses, he used to say."

That doesn't sound so bad to me.

"You wouldn't want to engulf my senses?"

"I thought I already did." He frowns.

"You do . . . I mean . . ." Oh shit, I think I just insulted him.

Kayne smiles down at me, clearly amused by my stupidity. "It's okay, kitten." He yanks me by the collar, forcing my face close to his. "You can have both of us under one condition."

"What's that?" I swallow roughly, caught up in the power of his gaze.

"You remember who you belong to when it's over."

"Like I could ever forget. Your palm print is permanently stamped on my ass."

"Damn straight." He spanks me hard, causing me to jerk. "Now lie on your stomach." He flips me over, still keeping a firm grip on my collar. "All this talk about threesomes and head and engulfing your senses has made me hard." He keeps my face planted on the pillow with one hand on my collar and pulls up my hips with the other. I instantly liquefy.

"Now fucking scream my name, kitten. So I know you'll never forget." With that, he slams into me, bucking me forward. *"Oh!"* I grab onto the edge of the mattress as his cock hits me square in my center, causing my muscles to coil around him like a snake.

"Who owns you, Ellie?" he asks as he beats into me from behind, my body completely subdued by his hold on my collar and hand clamped on my hip.

"You!" I exclaim as my pussy floods with forced arousal.

"And who am I?" he demands as our skin slaps together.

"My life, my love, my happiness!" I spout as he ruins me in the most delicious kind of way.

Kayne halts, buried deep inside me. "That's right, kitten." He leans over and murmurs in my ear, "Who else am I?"

I look up at him through the corner of my eye. "My owner. You own me." I speak the words he wants to hear.

"That's right, baby. Till death do us part."

I nod.

"Now tell me you love me."

"I love you," I proclaim with no hesitation. "Only you."

Kayne kisses my cheek affectionately then pulls out and re-positions me on my back. "I love you, too." He slides into me sweetly. "Only you." He looks directly into my eyes as I spread my legs, inviting him inside. "That's right, kitten, let me in." He sinks deeply into my channel, penetrating all the way to my core.

"Kayne," I moan, as he splits me open.

"Ellie." He exhales my name, the same need evident in his tone.

"Make me come," I implore, as he fucks me leisurely.

"You know I'll give you anything you want. I can never say no to you."

And that's the truth. Kayne would deny me very few things. An orgasm when I'm bad is one thing on that very short list, but right now, I could ask for the moon on a silver platter and he would find a way to bring it to me.

"Mmm." He closes his eyes and rests his forehead against mine as his cock thickens.

I run my hands through his dark brown hair as he rocks in

and out of me, both of us on a razor sharp edge about to topple over.

"Kayne." I whimper and shake as his body commands mine. *"Kayne!"* He thrusts in deep, shattering us both, the two of us moaning and panting and gyrating until the tumultuous ache subsides and all that's left in the climatic aftermath is two stripped bodies and a pile of bare bones.

Ruined . . .

I'm most definitely ruined.

ELLIE

IT'S DARK IN MY ROOM. The shadows on the wall look like blobs of moving ink as the clouds cover the moon and its white reflective light. Like every night, I wait anxiously for my owner. I sit on my knees chained to the bed, apprehensively expecting his arrival. I've fought him for so long, but tonight I will finally give in. Give in to him and the darkness. It will be my descent. The door creaks open and my body tenses. I keep my head down and listen to his footsteps. They sound different tonight. Lighter, but more ominous. When I look up, it isn't my owner standing in front of me, but it is a man I recognize. A man with a cold, calculating stare and unrepentant desires. A man who craves pain and delivers it explicitly. As soon as our eyes meet, I cower away, attempting to escape the impending doom. I know it's a vain effort, as he overtakes me every time.

"No!" I scream as he snatches my chain like lightning and yanks me toward him.

"That word doesn't exist in my world," he sneers. It's the same words every time. *"Bite me and I'll beat you unconscious."* Then I'm choking and crying and gagging all at the same time as he rams his cock mercilessly down my throat. Michael stands behind him laughing as I fruitlessly fight, knowing the torture is just beginning. Before I know it, I'm forced to my back, my throat raw and my voice hoarse from screaming. It just echoes around me, trapping me in. No one can hear me; no one can save me.

The first thrust feels like a serrated hot poker stabbing between my legs. The second scars me permanently. I kick and flail, but no amount of resistance will stop him. I know this. I have lived through this horror many times before.

"Stop!" I sob. "Stop! Stop!"

He laughs maniacally, reveling in my pain.

"Your pussy saves you every time." Michael's voice evaporates.

"ELLIE!" Kayne shakes me.

"Ellie, wake up!"

I gasp as I open my eyes to meet Kayne's worried blue ones. My stomach rolls. "Oh god, get off!" I push him then fly out of bed and into the bathroom, reaching the toilet bowl just in time. I throw up violently, purging the sickening feelings until my stomach is empty.

Kayne kneels on the floor beside me, holding my hair and rubbing my back as I dry heave uncontrollably.

When there's absolutely nothing left, I slump next to the toilet.

Kayne pulls me into his chest and presses my face against his warm skin.

"Shhhh." He pets my head and rocks me until I'm calm. I cling to him while the leftover bile burns my throat. "That hasn't happened to you in a long time."

"I know," I answer feebly as my body begins to relax.

"Was it me? Did I trigger it?" he asks worried, no doubt believing it was our bout of rough sex that brought on the dream.

"No," I say truthfully. I haven't had a violent nightmare about Javier and Michael in almost six months. But that doesn't mean what they did to me has vanished from my subconscious. I used to have that same dream all the time. Sometimes five nights in a row. When the hospital discharged me, I lost a considerable amount of weight because I puked every time I startled awake. The exact same way I did tonight.

"I'm fine." I wipe the tears from my face. "I just need some water." I try to smile, try to placate him, because the last thing I want is Kayne worrying that he's the cause of my recurring nightmares.

"C'mon." He lifts me to my feet and helps to steady me. Our bathroom is enormous so it takes several steps to get from the toilet bowl to the sink. The whole room is white marble with copper fixtures. It's a spa-like oasis with the shower and soaking tub overlooking the picturesque landscape.

I turn on the faucet and rinse my mouth with some cold water then swish some Scope around to kill the nasty vomit taste. Kayne stands by my side, his worried stare searing through the side of my head the whole time.

Once I dry my mouth, he pulls me next to him, so my side is touching his. We gaze at each other in the mirror as he raises the hem of my shirt—one of his white clingy undershirts that I've made a habit of living in. He only lifts it as far as my ribcage, exposing the circular tattoo that matches his. Around the scar where Michael shot me are the words *That which does not destroy us* written in fancy cursive. The same words circle Kayne's scar where Javier shot him in the shoulder. I know what he's trying to tell me. Fight. And I am. I have been for the last four years, and I'll continue to fight for the rest of my life. If I didn't, I wouldn't survive. And that's just not an option.

The tattoos were Kayne's idea. We got them on our first wedding anniversary. As a reminder, a symbol, a signification of strength. I've come to learn my husband loves philosophy, theology, and metaphysical poetry. He's filled our home office with works of Richard Crashaw, Friedrich Nietzsche, John Donne, and John Wesley. Apparently, Jett was the influence for Kayne's educational interests. When they first met, Kayne was a bit "rough around the edges." That's how Jett put it anyway, attempting to be sarcastic and empathetic all at the same time. Before Kayne met Jett, his reading material consisted of comic books and car magazines. The first book Jett ever gave him was the *Canterbury Tales,* and I quote, said, "Read it, Neanderthal." Kayne wasn't a fan at first, but somehow, Jett instilled a love for literature and philosophy in him.

"Are you sure you're okay?" Kayne asks, cutting through the severe silence.

I nod, resting my head against his arm. "I'm fine."

"I didn't trigger it?" Insecurity peeks through his stoic façade.

I stare at him in the mirror.

Well...not in the way he thinks. Kayne's dominant behavior didn't bring on the nightmare. I think his mention of kids did. He asked about starting a family a few days ago. No pressure, he was just poking around to see how I felt about it. I can tell you that I feel the same way as I did four years ago — resistant to the idea.

I'm not sure I want to disrupt the perfect little life we've carved out. And starting a family would definitely do that. Am I being selfish? Maybe. Do I have justification to feel that way? I think I do, given everything I've been through.

"No," I assure him once more. It's half the truth. "I'm ready to go back to bed."

"Okay." He kisses my head tentatively then walks me back into our bedroom with a death grip on my hand. Once under the covers, I cuddle up next to him, my body drawing calmness from his warmth. He's always warm and eager to hold me. I drift off listening to the sound of Kayne's breathing and the soft laps of the ocean just outside. I don't dream of Michael or Javier again. Instead, I dream of a young, dark-haired, green-eyed boy playing in the sand, calling out Mom.

ELLIE

"YOU ALMOST READY, KITTEN?" KAYNE asks, leaning against the doorframe of our office looking good enough to eat.

"I'm responding to my last email." I flick my eyes up at him.

And also responding to the way you look in those wind pants and tight t-shirt. Whoa.

Our foundation, and my current baby, has taken off tremendously. Over the last three years, we have sent nearly four hundred survivors and their families to all seven continents. I personally coordinate all the arrangements with the help of a local travel agent on Oahu. So many stories and so many survivors. I correspond with each and every one of them. My soul just floods with joy knowing that I'm providing someone with something they could only dream about. I dreamed of paradise for so long, and at one point even believed my hopes and aspirations were stolen away from me. Luckily, that wasn't the case, and I came away with more than I could have anticipated.

A husband who once told me he would kill for me, and then made good on his promise. A husband who gives me everything and asks only that I love him honestly in return, flaws and all. Which I do.

I'm compelled to share some of my good fortune, and through To Catch a Falling Star, I do. The foundation got its name from the tattoo scribbled on Kayne's rib cage, *A certain kind of darkness is needed to see the stars* and the knowledge of all those girls he saved from Javier's home. I think about them often, even though I never personally met any of them. I wonder if maybe one or two of them were part of the four hundred we've sent away thus far. A tiny piece of me hopes so.

I hit send, then push away from the desk. I've been plugging away at the computer since six a.m.

"Do you have everything you need?" I ask Kayne as we walk hand in hand down the curved staircase.

"Yup. Bottled water, snacks, and a hat."

"What about a compass?" I ask.

Kayne smiles. "Have that, too." He taps his chest, right where the brightly colored tattoo is inked over his heart. "It always brings me home. I just follow North."

He makes me grin like an idiot sometimes. On the needle pointing North is my name permanently written in small lettering. That's right. *I'm* home. Signed, sealed, and delivered.

Six months after Kayne and I got married, he and Jett left on one last mission; when they returned home, they both resigned from Endeavor. Although he was only gone a few days and in little to no danger, (his words though I'm still skeptical), it was trying. Very, very trying. Not knowing where he was or what he was doing. My imagination had a field day at my expense. I don't know how spouses of duty men and women do it. I was a nervous wreck until the minute he came home.

And as thrilled as I was that he decided to retire from the super-secret black op spy business, I sort of had a feeling his retirement would be short lived. And I was right because six months later, a knock came at the door. It was the commander of Honolulu SWAT. The same SWAT team Jett and Kayne worked with to save me. A few openings had 'materialized.' I use quotes because two positions were basically created specifically for them. Both Kayne and Jett said yes, and my husband went from nonexistent undercover operative to specialized service provider. AKA full-time, gun-toting, Kevlar-wearing badass.

Which, of course, he loves.

I sort of do, too. Especially when he walks around the house dressed in black fatigues with firearms holstered all over his body. *Hot.*

We climb into my Jeep. Not the one I used to drive, no. Kayne felt I needed an upgrade, so he purchased a new white Rubicon complete with body armor—a steel cage looking thing over the roof and front grille—for me. Boys and their toys. I end up driving the Jag half the time because he's always hogging the Wrangler.

We drive several blocks in the perfect October weather before we pull up to our destination. A large two-story house with a Chevelle parked in the driveway. We don't even bother knocking as we walk into Jett and London's home. They moved into the neighborhood shortly after Kayne and I did. It was sort of a whirlwind. Baby, house, marriage, in that order, but it was clear they couldn't be happier, despite London's horrific morning sickness.

"Peanut butter!" a high-pitched voice squeaks as soon as Kayne walks into the living room. Jett and London's house may be as large and spacious as ours is with the same panoramic view, but it feels much different with baby gates and toys tossed all around.

"Jelly!" Kayne lifts Layla as she runs and jumps into his arms. I don't exactly know where the nicknames came from, but they've been calling each other that since Layla could talk. "Pretty girl, what's all over your face?" he asks as he examines her.

"Makeup." She chortles like she knows she's not supposed to be wearing it but doesn't care.

"Yup, Jett caught her red handed playing in our bathroom," London says as she bounces six-month-old Beckett around on her hip, the newest member of the Fox household. "After he scolded her, he taught her how to apply blush. He's stealing all my thunder." She laughs.

"We were just having some daddy-daughter time," Jett announces as he comes down the stairs. He's dressed similar to Kayne in a white T-shirt, form-fitting hiking pants, and a pair of Ray Bans sitting on his blond head.

"Yeah, London, he needs his girl time or he'll lose all his estrogen," Kayne digs.

"What's esprjin?" Layla asks cheerfully.

We all erupt.

"It's your daddy's super power," Kayne tells her, highly amused.

"That's right." Jett tries to grab the gorgeous little blonde with her daddy's coloring and mommy's stunning face, but she latches onto Kayne's neck. Jett should know by now those two really are stuck together like peanut butter and jelly.

"Fine, then," he says to Layla, sticking out his tongue. She just laughs at him while holding Kayne tight.

"You're going to have to let go sooner or later." London delivers her the bad news as she puts Becks in his playpen. "Daddy and Uncle Kayne are going hiking."

"I wanna go!" She bops in Kayne's arms. "Please, please, please!"

Kayne and Jett throw a communicative look at each other.

"I don't have a problem with it." Kayne shrugs, more than happy to take her.

Jett huffs. "You really want to go?" he asks Layla directly.

"Yes, *pleassse*, Daddy?" Her turquoise eyes sparkle just like his.

"What do you think?" Jett consults London.

"It's fine with me. I just need to grab a hat and some sunscreen for her."

Let me tell you something. Kayne and Jett may think they run things, but this little girl rules the roost.

"I'll grab the carrier," Jett sighs, pretending to be annoyed. He pinches Layla's calf right before he walks out of the room. She giggles loudly in triumph.

As we wait for Jett to return, London grabs sunscreen from the bathroom and lathers Layla up. She then retrieves some snacks and a juice box from the kitchen just as Jett returns with a blue book bag looking thing.

"I want to go on Uncle Kayne's back!" Layla demands in a whiney tone.

"Fine with me," Jett agrees all too willingly.

"Of course, you can," Kayne placates her sweetly, resting his forehead against hers. "Your daddy couldn't carry a butterfly up a hill."

"I like butterflies."

"I know you do, pretty girl." He chuckles.

Jett leers at Kayne, "Aww, ffff . . . *Fudgesicle.*"

"I want a Fudgesicle!" Layla exclaims.

London and I can barely hold it together. The interaction

between the three of them is just too cute.

"Okay. Time to go." London starts ushering the two men and a little lady out.

Layla becomes excited. "I want to see fish! And a waterfall and a rainbow!"

"Whatever you want, jelly," Kayne appeases her as he carries her out the front door. "You can put in your full order in the car."

Yes, my heart actually skips a beat watching the two of them together.

"Have fun!" London yells. "Be careful! Jett, stay on the trail!"

I don't hear Jett's response clearly, but I think it was along the lines of "Yeah, yeah, woman, I know!"

Once gone, London shuts the door, turns around, and gives me a look. *That look.* Oh no, here it comes.

"That man needs a child." The words fly out of her mouth as if on cue.

"Please don't start," I implore her, instantly annoyed.

"I am just making an observation," she defends her statement.

"You've been making that observation a lot lately."

"I can't help what I see."

I lean on the kitchen island and stare at London. "I'm just not sure."

She dispenses a sympathetic look. "I know the subject of family is between you and Kayne, but Ellie, just tell me what you're afraid of."

It takes me a few moments to answer her, as I try to put my feelings into words. "Everything."

"Everything?" She crosses her arms confounded. "Do you think you're going to be a bad mother?"

"Compared to you, maybe," I joke.

"Ellie."

"No, it's not that." I wrap my arms around myself. "I just know what's out there. I don't want what happened to me to happen to my children."

London's face drops. "Oh, Ellie."

I wipe my eye, a rebel tear forming in the corner.

"I didn't mean to upset you."

"I know." I try to smile. "I just don't know how you do it."

London moves closer to me until our bodies are touching. She plays with the ends my hair and looks at me sympathetical- ly. "I wish I could give you a guarantee. I wish I could tell you that everything will always be perfect, but I think you're smart enough to know that's not true."

"You could lie to me."

"I could, but I won't. What I will tell you is that you have an advantage."

"Advantage?"

"Yup. You know what's out there. You can recognize the danger and teach your children the signs. If you ever decide to have any." She winks. "We've all been through our own trau- matic shit. But the way I see it, if you let it get in the way of your happiness, you're letting it win."

She does have a point. And London has lived through her own personal hell, one that was way longer and way worse than mine, and she's not letting it hold her back.

Are my negative experiences holding me back? Am I mak- ing excuses because of my fear? Maybe. Or maybe I've already committed myself to someone and I'm not ready to share him yet. Maybe, I'm scared it will change what we have. And like I've said before, I really love *us*.

"Whatever you decide, I'll support you. I just don't want you look back and have regrets."

"I don't want that, either." I also don't want to deprive my husband of something he really wants.

"Good." London walks out of the kitchen to check on Becks, who's been extremely quiet.

"God, I love this child," I hear her say.

"Why?" I peek into the living room to see Becks cuddled up in the corner of his playpen fast asleep.

"Because he's such a man. Eat, sleep, poop. That's his life."

"At six months old, what more do you need?"

"Nothing." She smiles down at the little towhead. He, too, got his father's coloring, but his mommy's dark blue eyes.

"So . . . speaking of men, do you think you can get Malia to babysit overnight next weekend?" I decide now is as good a time as any to change the subject.

London snaps her head up. "I'm sure I can, why?"

I smile, unable to hide my excitement. "Kayne said yes."

Her eyes widen to the size of satellites. "You got him to agree?"

"Yes!" The rock in the pit of my stomach does a summersault. "Do you suddenly have a problem with me sleeping with your husband?"

London and I have talked about this. Extensively. She knows how much I want to be with both Kayne and Jett and has been nothing but supportive.

"No." She tiptoes away from Beckett quietly and directs me back to the kitchen. "I slept with your husband. It's only fair. Just be prepared. I've been the filling in that alpha sandwich."

"I know." I pout. "And I'm tired of living vicariously through you."

"Apparently, you won't have to much longer."

ELLIE

WE WATCH AS THE LAST bits of daylight fade away, casting a grayish-blue hue on the ocean and mountainous landscape. Jett, London, Kayne, and I have just finished a dinner on the lanai of grilled steak, mashed potatoes, and sautéed asparagus. I swallow the last of my wine before I start clearing the table.

"Do you want some help, Ellie?" London asks, moving to stand.

"I'm fine." I motion for her to sit. "You clean up twenty-four hours a day."

"That isn't a lie." She smiles as she sinks back into her chair. I pile the plates and bring them into the kitchen as Kayne scrubs the grill and Jett irritates him by pointing out all the spots he missed. I laugh to myself while rinsing the dishes, highly amused by the three people I love in each their own way. After loading the dishwasher, I jump when I feel Jett standing behind me.

"Jesus!"

"Nope, just Jett." He grins. I swear he and Kayne can be silent as shadows when they want to be. "Silverware?" He holds up a handful of forks and knives.

"Just stick them in the sink," I instruct as I head to the refrigerator. I hear the metal clink behind me.

"Any dessert?" Jett asks, curiously. When he and London come over, I always know to have dessert. He has one wicked sweet tooth.

"Of course." I pull out a cake from the fridge. "Red velvet."

I place it on the counter in front of him and remove the

Saran Wrap. I then swipe my finger in the icing and hold it up to him. "The cream cheese frosting is even homemade, especially for you."

Jett stares down at my finger, a small little smirk playing on his lips. "You know it's not nice to tease me, Ellie."

I step closer to him. "Who's teasing?"

Jett's mouth falls slightly open. It's not often he's surprised, but when he is, it's a classic moment. I watch closely as he glances outside to see Kayne's reaction. He's just standing casually next to London, the two of them voyeurs to our little show. He nods at Jett, as if giving him the okay.

"You sure about this?" Jett asks, bringing his attention back to me, his turquoise eyes now wild and alight.

"Yes," I answer confidently.

"You know once we start, there's no stopping." Jett wraps one of his hands around mine, bringing my frosting covered finger to his lips. "Are you ready for that?"

I swallow thickly, staring directly into Jett's eyes. I nod, the heat coming on faster than I anticipated.

"You're blushing, sweet thing." Jett slips my finger into his mouth and swirls his tongue around the tip. My knees go weak. "Answer me, Ellie," Jett urges. "Are you ready?"

"Yes," I breathe out. "I know exactly who I belong to."

Jett smirks fiendishly. "After tonight, you may reconsider that."

"Don't make me kill you." Kayne's voice cuts through the sexual tension smothering the room. I glance over to see him and London on the other side of the breakfast bar and wonder idly how long they've been standing there. "I don't feel like looking for a new best friend."

"In situations like these, you know I have no control over the outcome," Jett taunts him.

They share a silent exchange before Jett asks outright, "Are you okay with this?"

Kayne sighs, relenting, "What my kitten wants, she gets."

"And your kitten wants me?" Jett responds, gratified, almost triumphant.

"I want both of you," I clarify.

"Then both of us you shall have." With that, he swiftly

scoops me up and throws me over his shoulder.

I squeal instinctively.

Jett makes it upstairs in record time, Kayne and London hot on his heels. Once in the master bedroom, he tosses me onto the bed. "Stay," he orders as Kayne pins me with a heated stare.

I glance over at London, worried and disheveled on the bed. She communicates silently, *you asked for this, be prepared.* She did warn me numerous times that taking on Kayne and Jett is like trying to tame two wild animals. But the warning always excited me more than scared me. Except now, about to be in the thick of it, I wonder if I'm biting off more than I can chew.

I guess I'll soon find out.

"London, undress Ellie." The command comes swiftly from Jett, like a hard slap. She moves quickly, pulling my jean skirt down. She then pulls me up and rips off my tank top. In five seconds flat, I'm naked in front of the three of them.

"Thank you," Jett kisses her promptly on the cheek as she steps back between the four starving eyes raking over my bare body.

"Up." Jett crooks a finger at me.

I crawl to the edge of the bed and sit on my knees. I'm suddenly shaking. Tonight is going to be completely different. Different than any other time the four of us have shared. There are no boundaries tonight, no invisible line forbidden to cross. No more imagining . . . only experiencing. I steal a look at Kayne. He's cool and collected on the outside, but I wonder what he's feeling on the inside. His majestic blue gaze gives nothing away except fanatical lust.

"Be a good kitten and sit still," Jett instructs as he reaches over and grabs my collar, which is peeking out from under our pillows. Kayne likes to keep it chained to the vining iron headboard, right along with me. Jett fastens the white leather around my neck as I regard him curiously. He's never referred to me as kitten before, directly or indirectly. Kayne is the only one who has ever used my pet name. It feels strange and completely unlawful. But that is the whole point of tonight, breaking the rules of attraction. Jett smirks as if registering my silent thought. Once finished with my collar, he slides his hand into my hair and yanks firmly, tipping my face up. "Kayne may own you," he murmurs, his warm breath tickling the shell of my ear, "but a little piece of you has always belonged to me."

I sit like a statue processing his bold statement, agreeing with him beyond reason. Jett always has been an exotic spice in mine and Kayne's mix. "Tonight, you're our pet," he announces, jerking on my chain. The word *our* is not lost on me; it refers to all three people in this room. "I want to watch you pleasure my little bird, and if she isn't satisfied, you're going to get punished." Jett's lips curve up as mine turn down. He's never threatened to punish me before. I look at Kayne. He just shrugs a shoulder, as if agreeing with Jett. This is an odd, new dynamic. I don't know what I was expecting going into this, but being a shared pet with the threat of punishment definitely wasn't it.

"How do you answer, kitten?" Kayne's voice is hard, rough, dusted with desire.

"Yes, Jett," I answer obediently.

"Good girl." There's an air about Jett that I've never experienced before. It's commanding and authoritative, but not like the Jett I know. This person in front of me is someone else completely; this person is a huntsman, a skilled, cunning individual who appreciates the chase as much as the kill. I see it reflecting in his turquoise eyes. Eyes that have only shown flickers of the man who lurks beneath the surface.

London crawls onto the bed and kneels right in front of me. Even she is different tonight. There is not a blip of submissive energy radiating from her. Tonight, she's an equal to Kayne and Jett. It's sexy and intimidating all at the same time. She stares at my mouth, knowing full well what it's capable of, and eager for me to put it to good use.

"Undress me, kitten." Being called by my pet name by others sends a chill right down my spine. I never knew it could affect me in such a way, making me feel totally bound while at the same time so completely free.

I grab the hem of her loose fitting sundress and run my fingers along her skin as I pull it up. She's not wearing anything underneath, except a skimpy, bright orange thong. Once off, she tugs on my collar, bringing our faces close together. She's controlling the show, kissing me how she wants and where she wants. My lips, my cheeks, my neck, moving down until she reaches my breasts, biting and licking my nipples while Kayne and Jett watch fixated.

"I want your tongue all over me," London hisses in my ear, as she leans backward, pulling me along with a firm grip on my collar. She lies on her back, situating me directly on top of her. With an iron-clad grasp, she leads my face to her neck. Like instructed, I begin to lick. I run my tongue over her collarbone, down the center of her chest, until I reach her naked breasts, I tease each nipple with a slash of my tongue and suck hard, nipping her the way she did to me not moments ago. She moans audibly as she yanks on my collar, drawing me further down her body. She wants my mouth on her pussy; there's no disputing it. London is always greedy when it comes to me. She likes me one place, and that's with my head right between her thighs. I yank off her panties, nearly ripping them from excitement. Just as I take my first lick of her slit, I feel the bed dip both in front of me and behind me. My defenses instantly fly up. Shit's about to get real. I flick my eyes up to see Jett in front of me, leaning over London's outstretched body and feel Kayne's hands caressing the small of my back.

"Don't stop," Jett instructs as he presses his lips to London's arched chest. I keep up a fluid rhythm with my tongue as he moves down her body, following the same path I took seconds ago. I watch engrossed as he pulls each of her nipples into his mouth, stretching skin then moving down to her torso. He never takes his sharp turquoise stare off me as he comes closer, closer until his mouth is a breath away from mine. London squirms and moans beneath us, as I continually skim over her clit. Then it happens, Jett lashes out his tongue, simultaneously French kissing us both. The contact sends a heat wave through my whole body, blowing the doors of exhilaration wide open, desire and want running rampant through my entire nervous system.

London expels a low, throaty moan as the two of us begin to pleasure her, dueling tongues brushing over her fiery flesh and against each other. It's impossible not to lose myself at the moment, not to let the arousal take over and become my ruler. All at once, London rushes to her peak, Jett grabs a fistful of my hair, and Kayne sinks a finger into my entrance. With a controlling grip, Jett secures my face against London's pussy as

Kayne smears my wetness up away from my folds, and teases the tight ring of muscle over and over with his thumb.

"Make her come, Ellie," Jett demands between licks, his long flat tongue lapping up my saliva and the juices of London's excitement. Subdued in place, I suck and circle and stab at London's pussy as Kayne penetrates both my holes, priming and stretching, driving me completely insane.

"Oh, god!" London squirms like a fish. "I'm going to come! I'm going to come!" she exclaims in distress. "Fuck, you're both going to make me come!" She rocks her pussy against my face as a sudden rush of heat saturates my lips.

"Lick it up, Ellie. Suck up every single drop." Jett's voice is stern, commanding. His hold on my hair unyielding as I do as I'm told, consuming every droplet of desire that's threatening to drown me. Once her tremors subside and she's moaning languidly, Jett jerks my head up and smothers me with a kiss, his tongue aggressively claiming my mouth, the urgency nearly stealing my breath away.

"Good, kitten," he patronizes once we break apart. I look up at him winded as Kayne continues to finger me, scissoring open my rosebud as wide as my muscles will allow. I groan as he pushes past the point of pleasure. "We need you loose, baby," I hear Jett say as he lifts a limp and sated London off the bed and deposits her on the curved chaise on the opposite side of the room. "Be a good little bird and watch." He kisses her, sucking her bottom lip between his teeth.

"Yes, Jett," she purrs euphorically.

With that, he returns to the bed, shedding his clothes on the way. First, he tears off his T-shirt exposing his chiseled chest, nipple ring, and bright wavelike tattoos. Second, he unbuckles his belt like a man who knows exactly how to wield it, then drops his pants. Jett's nipple isn't the only part of his body that's pierced. Through his foreskin, a metal barbell with two large balls protrudes right under the head of his penis. It's one of the hottest things I have ever seen and when my tongue grazed it for the first time, I nearly expired. Since then, I've been aching to know what it feels like inside me. My mouth goes dry as he climbs onto the mattress, the hunter finally cornering his prey.

Kayne lifts me from all fours by my collar, the chain attached to the headboard straining as far as it can go. In a blink, I'm sandwiched between two solid bodies, four hands touching me, two mouths devouring me, and two pulsing cocks gunning for my pleasure. I don't know where or who to touch first, so I just try and keep up as Kayne twists my head to kiss me while Jett fondles my breasts and bites my neck. The sensations come on like a tornado—angst, lust, desire, need—all engulf me as I'm pushed and pulled, grabbed, fingered, and squeezed.

"It's your turn, little girl," Jett growls as he holds his hand over mine and jerks on his cock, showing me exactly how he likes it. Before I know it, I'm being positioned back on all fours, Kayne detaining my hips and Jett holding my chin.

"Open. Wide." He pokes the head of his erection against my lips and I open like instructed. He slowly slides his cock into the recesses of my mouth; the odd sensation of metal scraping against my tongue from his piercing again tickles my gag reflex.

"That mouth of yours is so good, Ellie." He pumps several greedy times before pulling out. "But that's not where I'm coming tonight," he tells me as he moves aside, allowing Kayne to push me forward onto my stomach.

"Over," Kayne orders with a slap on my ass. I roll onto my back, catching sight of him shedding his clothes. He moves differently than Jett, more rugged and rough. One a skilled hunter; the other a savage predator. Once his shirt and pants are gone, he covers my naked body with his, pressing me into the mattress, kissing my mouth rapturously and touching my body gluttonously. He twists one of my nipples and I release a muffled whimper.

"One of my favorite sounds," Kayne remarks as he pushes himself up, then manhandles me so I am lying directly on top of him, my back against his front. It's crystal clear that I have no say in what goes on here. My body belongs to them, and they will use it and abuse it exactly how they see fit.

Jett grabs my hands and pins them over my head. "This is our body tonight." He articulates my silent thoughts.

My anxiety spikes as he secures my wrists with the chain in an iron-clad binding. My heart pounds and my thighs tremble as Jett spreads my legs and Kayne nestles his rock-solid cock in the crack of my ass. "You ready, kitten?" Kayne asks as he nips on my earlobe and massages my breasts.

I can't even respond; the anticipation and fear have swallowed my voice. I'll be lucky to force a moan out. "I think she is." Jett ogles my naked, outstretched body, currently being served up specifically for him. "Just know, Ellie . . ." Jett slips his tongue into my ear and I shiver. "I have fantasized about tasting you here." He licks between my lips. "And here." He skims his finger over my soaking wet slit as he moves his tongue in slow circles around my mouth. "And when I take you," his voice is drenched with desire, "I'm not going to hold back."

There's something about Jett's tone — it's a hundred-proof cocktail made up of a warning, a threat, and a promise. Like all the delicious and frightening things he's capable of are about to rain down directly on top of me.

Jett swiftly kisses his way along my body, wasting no time tasting all the places he's fantasized about. When buries his face between my legs, it has a galvanic effect and I nearly convulse.

His tongue, oh Jesus, his tongue and the way he bends and curves it. The way he sucks and strikes and skims has me writhing, has me pulling on my restraints and moaning out loud.

"You like that, kitten?" Kayne rasps in my ear as he holds me still. "You like the way Jett eats *my* pussy?"

Again, I can't respond because I am caught in this alternate universe of pleasure. I merely mewl, detached as Jett licks me senseless.

"Answer him, kitten." Jett flicks my clit with his fingers, electrocuting my nerve endings. "Do you like the way I eat *his* pussy?"

I huff and puff, not answering fast enough, and Jett flicks my clit harder this time, causing me to cry out.

"Yes!" I pant, "Yes, I like the way you eat my pussy."

"Whose pussy?" Kayne bites my shoulder so hard I know I'm going to have a mark. "Your pussy!" I correct myself.

"That's right, kitten. Never forget it." He runs his tongue over my broken skin, lapping up the dewy drops of blood.

"No," I whimper illogically as Jett uses his fingertip to caress my throbbing clit. This whole situation is making me so crazy and so wet my arousal is literally dripping down my slit, and I haven't even climaxed yet.

"Something else belongs to me, too," Kayne says as he lifts my hips and pokes the head of his cock against my little puckered hole. "Stay still." He holds onto me firmly as he works his erection into my ass. Despite my evenly split moans of protest and pleasure, he continues his backdoor assault, sliding four inches in and two inches out over and over until he fully penetrates me. A small sheen of sweat covers my body as I breathe through the initial bites of discomfort. In this position, I am overly stretched, overly subdued, and overly vulnerable.

"My turn." Jett climbs on top of me and I become a bundle of nerves, so turned on and so unsure of what to expect. "Look at me, Ellie." The way he says my name, the way he grabs my chin and forces me to look him in the eyes, I nearly disintegrate. It's too exposing, too intense. I don't think I can handle it. I shut my eyes, but he grips me tighter and shakes my face. "Look. At. Me." He doesn't say it with anger; he says it with authority. He says it like he wants me to experience exactly what he's experiencing. I open my eyes when I feel his cock swimming through my soaked folds. My breath catches and then completely evaporates when he slides into me — slowly, leisurely, indulgingly — his gaze bestial as he fills me completely, the barbell through his foreskin stroking the walls of my channel, making the sensations that much more powerful. I've never felt anything like it. So filled, so stretched, so aroused, so desperate.

"Oh, god." I drop my head and tense in my restraints as they start to move, start to use me exactly how they want to, as a vessel for inconceivable pleasure.

Almost instantly, my body responds, begging to come. I try to contain it, but being engulfed in the heat of their bodies is enough to make me melt.

"Come," I distantly hear Kayne order me. "Come all over Jett's cock so he knows just how good you feel." He thrusts up into my ass just as Jett pulls out of my pussy. I nearly see stars, my insides crackling like live wires.

"Come, kitten." I hear the strain in his voice as he pulls on my collar.

"Yeah, come, kitten," Jett mimics Kayne's words and actions, thrusting into me while gripping my collar. I'm already trembling under a constellation of sensations when Kayne reaches around and rubs my clit. It feels like he hit a panic button as all of my senses go haywire. My vision blinks in and out as an unstoppable orgasm hits me like a wrecking ball. There's no stopping the shudders or the wracking or the coiling of my muscles around the two cocks buried deep inside me, reaping every single ounce of my pleasure. Demanding it. Sucking it straight from my core until there's nothing left to give. Until I'm only a languid mass sandwiched between two of the most intoxicating men I have ever met.

Mentally removed, I hear Jett and Kayne moan in my ear as they put their hands all over me, massaging my stressed limbs and taking advantage of my tethered state.

One, I'm not sure which, unbinds my wrists. My eyes are closed and I'm zapped of energy so I just let them do what they want, pulling out of me and flipping me over so I am now chest to chest with Kayne.

"Hi, kitten." He traps my head and kisses me. "Feeling okay?" he asks haughtily. He's enjoying this, I think, more than either of us expected.

I just grunt in response, attempting to cuddle up and fall asleep in his arms.

"We're not through yet," he informs me as he runs his hands down my sides and grabs both of ass cheeks.

"I told you there was a certain place I wanted to come," Jett murmurs behind me. His heated skin pressing against my own. "Let me in." He rubs his still erect cock between my cheeks as Kayne spreads them open.

"Let us both in." They simultaneously move to enter me. Kayne first, sliding into my pussy easily, while Jett works his way into my already exploited buttonhole. My womb knots like a twisted rope as I'm filled again, my body bowed in the new position.

"Come with us, Ellie." Kayne threads his fingers in my hair and grabs hold, keeping my face an inch away from his. He licks and bites on my bottom lip as the two of them let loose, fucking me hard, pursuing their own pleasure. "Come on, baby, come." Kayne thrusts at the same time as Jett and my body locks up.

"No," I plead. I don't think I can survive another earth-shattering quake like the one before.

"Yes."

"I can't." I strain as their cocks swell inside me, close to the brink.

"You can, and you will, because we say so."

"No." I nearly cry as one of them rubs my clit, adamantly, unforgivingly.

"Yes." Jett pulls my head back and kisses me, plunging his tongue into my mouth the same way he's plunging his cock into my ass.

"Come." My clit is rubbed harder, my nipples are teased and I'm filled to the brim as I dance the darkest rhythm of my life. Then it happens, an orgasm snowballs inside me, growing larger and larger with every strike and stroke and pinch until there's no stopping it. Until the demands on my body win out and my core catches fire and burns me alive.

I scream into Jett's mouth as I'm thoroughly fucked. Fucked until I go slack and the two men controlling me come. Come in my bruised, sore, supremely satisfied body.

Holy mother of God.

The last thing I remember is being cocooned in a blanket of warmth, heavy breathing, and soft lingering kisses, right before I pass out cold.

I WAKE UP TO THE sound of laughter echoing faintly through the house and the smell of coffee. I sit up in bed, my aching body protesting as I stretch my arms and legs. I'm still chained to the headboard; there are bruises on my hips and a bite mark on my shoulder. I look like a wreck, but I feel completely blissful. I unbuckle my collar and slink out of bed. Holy shit, I'm sore from tip to tip between my legs. I hobble into the bathroom to brush my teeth then throw on a pair of shorts and a tank top. I'm just at the top of the stairs when Kayne comes bounding up. When my eyes meet his, I suddenly blush, unexpectedly self-conscious.

"Hey." He cups my face and gives me a kiss.

"Hey," I respond shyly. Why am I uncomfortable? This is my husband.

"Why are you so red?" he asks curiously.

Because you shared me with your best friend last night and I'm not sure how I feel about it.

Or how you feel about it.

I shrug in response. "Do you still love me?" I wonder out loud.

"Ellie?" Kayne is thoroughly amused. "Why would you ask something so ridiculous?"

"Because of last night?"

"You think I'm mad?"

I shrug again, attempting to be cute and, well, tempting. "Do I sound mad?"

I shake my head.

"Do I look mad?"

I shake my head once more. He actually looks refreshed and very happy.

"Then there's your answer."

"Did you enjoy it?" I can't help but ask. I have to know.

Kayne looks at me impishly. "Let's just say I was hoping you were still sleeping so I could wake you up with my tongue." He takes my hand and puts it between his legs so I feel his stiff erection.

"You liked it that much?"

Kayne nods, his eyes on fire. "I think the four of us have turned a corner in our sexual relationship."

My jaw drops. "Are you being serious? You'd do it again?"

"Again and so much more."

"More?" I repeat.

"Mmm hmm." He drops a kiss on my lips. "We can talk about *more,* later. London and Jett are getting ready to leave. Come say good-bye." He leads me down the stairs into the kitchen. That same sense of self-consciousness resurfaces when I come face to face with Jett. What the hell is wrong with me?

"Well, Sleeping Beauty finally decided to wake up," he comments as he takes a sip of coffee.

I regard him silently as heat creeps up over my cheeks. All I can picture is him naked, tattooed, and pierced. *Not good.* I need to get a grip.

I grab a coffee mug and pour myself a cup, finally mustering enough nerve to answer him.

"A girl needs her caffeine fix."

"That's not the only fix a girl needs." Jett pokes fun at me. I could smack him.

I roll my eyes in response instead. "And she got it."

I throw a glance at London, and she winks. Yes, the four of us have a weird dynamic, but it works.

London's phone chirps on the counter, and she hurries to check it. "Layla is asking for us, *again*."

Jett takes one more large gulp of coffee. "That's our cue." He and London stand up. Adult swim is over for them.

Jett and London walk around the breakfast bar to say their goodbyes. London breezily kisses me on the cheek, like nothing unusual occurred at all. Like, I didn't just sleep with her husband last night.

"Watching you with Jett was one of the hottest things I have ever seen," she whispers in my ear. "And you know I have seen a lot."

That she has. Probably more than any one person should see in a lifetime.

"Really?" I respond quietly, almost timid.

She nods, her dark-blue eyes sparkling perversely. London is always the picture of perfection outside the bedroom door. But behind it, her multifaceted persona peeks through. Her fiendish, fearless, provocative side.

When Jett hugs me, several emotions stir simultaneously— excitement, embarrassment, and a calming affection. It's obvious I wasn't prepared for the impact of last night, although it seems like I'm the only one who's rattled.

"You know what, Ellie?" Jett speaks softly as he embraces me.

"What?"

"You really do taste like cupcakes," he whispers in amusement.

I reply with a small gasp. Kayne must be sharing our secrets. He always tells me I taste like cupcakes.

Jett kisses me on the cheek, a firm, wet, sloppy gesture before he takes London by the hand and leaves.

ELLIE

LONDON AND I HAVE ALTERNATED hosting Thanksgiving for the last four years, and this year it's my turn. The house smells amazing. I made my mother's sweet potato pie, my grandmother's stuffing, and cooked a turkey big enough to feed twelve.

"Kayne!" I yell into the living room. "Can you come in here and help me with this monstrosity of a bird you made me buy!" Yes, the turkey was all him. He wanted leftovers . . . for a month. I swear the man eats like a racehorse. I always joke that I need a part-time job just to pay the grocery bill.

"Coming!" He walks into the kitchen holding Layla under his arm like a football.

"Now how are you supposed to help me when your arms are full?" I joke, tapping Layla's little nose. She giggles.

"Only one arm is full." He squeezes her and she squeaks. "I still have this one." He grabs one of the oven mitts off the counter. "If I can bench press you with one hand, I can pull a thirty-pound turkey out the oven."

I don't have a second to respond before London swoops in and slips Layla out from under Kayne's arm. "I'll take her. We'll just stand over here and watch." She steps back behind the island.

"Fair enough." Kayne grabs the other oven mitt and pulls the turkey from the oven. It looks so perfect I almost squeal. I don't know when I became so domestic, but seeing that beautiful brown bird come out of the oven gives me chills.

Kayne carves it and I place it on the set table. Not two seconds after he sits down, Layla is off her chair and climbing onto his lap. London scolds her but she insists, refusing to eat unless she stays put.

"It's fine," Kayne smoothes his hand over Layla's blonde hair. "She can eat wherever she wants."

Sucker.

"You spoil her," London scolds *him* now.

Kayne just shrugs. "My house, my rules."

I just shake my head, laughing internally. How many times have I heard that?

Everyone begins to make their plates while talking and passing and sampling. This is Becks' first Thanksgiving, so we all get to experience his first taste of turkey. He doesn't seem like a fan; he just keeps throwing it on the floor.

Just as we all begin to eat, Jett raises his wine glass. "A toast."

With the fork a few inches from his mouth, Kayne groans. "Really? Every time?"

I nudge him with my foot under the table, reminding him of his manners. Sometimes he forgets. As much as he looks like a well-groomed adult, he can sometimes act like a surly teenager.

"Go ahead," I encourage Jett.

"I'll make this short and sweet." He glares at Kayne. If there weren't children at the table, I know what Kayne's choice response to that look would be. "I just wanted to thank Ellie for this wonderful meal and say I am grateful for all the past holidays we have spent at this table and am looking forward to many more. Cheers."

"Cheers," the rest of us respond.

"See? Short."

"And very sweet," I add.

Kayne snorts. "Wonderful. Can we eat now?"

"By all means, savage." Jett facetiously grants permission.

Kayne scoops an oversized forkful of mashed potatoes into his mouth then smiles condescendingly at Jett. *Boys.*

The rest of dinner sails by with an abundance of laughter and energy. Both children, the stars of the show. Layla sings and plays with her food on Kayne's lap while Becks keeps London busy with smeared mashed potatoes and squished turkey.

"You know what you're eating?" Kayne asks Layla as she pops her peas into her mouth, one by one.

"A pea!" she enthusiastically answers, holding up the little green ball.

"Nuh-uh."

"Uh-huh!" She's adamant.

"Lizard poop," he tells her.

"Ewww!"

"Kayne!" Jett admonishes. "Do you have any idea how long it took us to get her to eat peas? They're the only vegetable she'll eat!"

"Not anymore." Kayne laughs as Layla pushes her peas around on her plate like they're contaminated with something.

"Are they really lizard poop, Daddy?"

"No, honey. They come out of the pod, remember? Mommy and I showed you. Uncle Kayne is just teasing."

"Oh, yeah! I remember!" Her turquoise eyes shine brightly.

I won't lie and say my heart doesn't melt seeing Kayne with Layla, watching her happily feed him lizard poop and him happily eating it.

London's words haven't stopped ringing in my ears all night. *That man needs a child.*

Deep down—very far down—I know that she's right. I know he wants one desperately. I also know my reservations and fears shouldn't stop us from having a family, but they are.

After dessert is served, the table is cleared, and the children have fallen asleep, London and Jett call it a night. Layla passed out in Kayne's arms while he and Jett watched football on the couch.

I've already started on the dishes when Kayne comes back inside from walking London and Jett out. He wraps his arms around my waist and hugs me affectionately with his chin resting on my shoulder. We stand like that for several minutes as I continually rinse each plate.

"It's quiet now," he states.

"What's quiet?" I ask.

"The house. It's quiet now with everyone gone."

I stop and listen. It definitely is.

"Maybe it's time we fill it up," I say delicately, drying my hands with a dishtowel. I feel Kayne's arms tighten before he spins me around.

"Fill it up?"

"Yeah," I answer coyly. "Maybe it's time we start a family of our own." It's an impulsive decision because that's how I do things, but it feels like the right one.

My heart beats erratically as Kayne just stands there and stares at me. I think I just shocked him. Actually, I know I did.

"Are you being serious?"

"Yes," I answer pointedly. "And a lot of things are going to have to change around here if we have a baby. Our lifestyle, namely."

Kayne grins deviously. "We can cross that bridge when we come to it. Jett and London make it work. We can, too."

They definitely do. If I have learned anything from the two of them, it's that you don't stop being who you are just because you start a family. If anything, you hold on tighter to the person you were, somehow incorporating your old life with your new one.

"How soon can you stop your birth control?" Kayne asks excitedly.

"I'm supposed to go for a shot next month. I can skip it."

"A month, huh?" I can see the wheels turning. "That gives us time to practice."

"Practice for what?"

"Making babies." He grabs my neck and crushes his mouth against mine. The kiss consumes me, stealing my essence right out of me. We kiss and kiss, our tongues tangling as our hands roam all over each other.

"I say we start practicing right now." He grazes his teeth along my neck then bites my earlobe.

"No time like the present." I moan as he caresses me between my legs, over the fabric of my jeans.

"Let's go." He hauls me off the ground, encouraging me to lock my legs around his waist. I grind on his cock the whole way to our room, expecting him to toss me on the bed, but he apparently has other ideas as he walks us into our playroom.

"Take your clothes off," he orders as he drops me in front of the swing. My arousal skyrockets. His dominance will always be my undoing. Kayne watches as I pull each piece of clothing off. My white gauzy shirt, my Capri jeans, and boy short underwear. The ones made entirely of hot pink lace. Almost immediately, I'm completely naked while he is still fully dressed.

He sighs appreciatively as he gropes my breasts, teases my nipples, and consumes my mouth, stretching it wide as he forcefully circles his tongue. I can't help but whimper, knowing full well the assault he's about to launch on my body.

He lifts me into the harness, two thick nylon straps supporting me, one under my butt the other behind my back. On each of the four straps hanging from the ceiling are wrist and ankle cuffs, which Kayne wastes no time buckling me into. Once tethered, he stalks around me, the spider inspecting his spun-up prey. I see the lust illuminating in his eyes as he runs one finger along the inside of my outstretched thighs.

I have no idea what he's planning; the only thing I can be sure of is that this isn't going to be a straight-up fuck. He wants to play. And I'm the toy.

"Comfortable?" He strums my clit.

"I'd be more comfortable with you inside me," I tell him point blank. I want him to fuck me and fuck me right now. Those soft, light caresses are eliciting a slow burn from the inside out.

"Soon enough." He walks away, out of sight. Kayne purposely keeps our treasure chest in a corner of the room I can't see. He likes to surprise me. He likes to be in complete control. And I don't just mean control of my body. He likes to mess with my mind and trifle with my desire. While I hang here helpless, the room suddenly goes black as Kayne ties a silk blindfold around my head. After he tightens it, he murmurs in my ear, "Beautifully bound, exactly how I like you." I feel him tickle the diamond heart hanging on my choker. One of his many symbols of ownership over me. Maybe the most significant.

I then feel him nudge something against my entrance. It's hard and thick and penetrates me fully. With a click, the vibrator hums to life, waking up every single one of my nerve endings. "Oh." I shudder with need, but the soft buzz only teases me. There's not nearly enough vibration to bring me close to the edge.

"Hang around, kitten. I'll be back." There's amusement and

excitement in Kayne's voice as I catch the sound of strange clicks in the darkness.

Strapped in the swing, I have no choice but to do as he says while my arousal slowly stifles me like smoke. The light buzz kindling my excitement while suppressing it all at the same time. I fuss helplessly, knowing Kayne will only return when *he's* ready. I try to concentrate on the shower running when I begin to smell a spicy blend of cinnamon, vanilla, and nutmeg in the room. I don't know how long I'm alone, but the wait is excruciating as my need curls around my limbs and weighs me down.

"Miss me, kitten?" Kayne says suddenly.

"Yes," I answer, wanting.

"Yes, what?" He snaps something against my nipple and I flinch.

"Yes, Kayne." I grit my teeth.

"Good girl. Just because we are preparing for things to change doesn't mean they have yet." He flicks my nipple again with what I think is the towel, and it bites me harder this time. "Yes, Kayne!" My voice pitches from the pain.

"Mmm . . . those word from your lips." I feel the straps by my hands strain and the weight of my husband against me. "I'll never get tired of hearing you say them. I'll never get tired of hearing you beg. You will always be mine." He nips at my bottom lip, but that's all I get of him. "I'll never, ever let you go."

"I don't ever want you to let me go," I rasp, feeding off his energy.

"Good." With that, I feel the first burn against my skin, a fiery line across my lower abdomen. I squeal in surprise. Wax, hot wax. That's what the spicy smell was, a burning candle. It cools quickly, hardening on my torso. I only have a second of reprieve before I feel it again. This time the fiery trail moves upwards on my stomach, some drips are bigger than others, but they all light my body on fire the same way. I squirm when he covers one of my nipples, the little nub baking under the heat.

"Oh, god." He does the same to the other breast, the wax dripping down my side, reaching all the way to my back. I'm caught between a constant state of kindle and flame. The vibrator tortures the inside of my body while the hot wax does a number on the outside. I drop my head back as I feel him make his way up my chest and stop just below my necklace.

"Hold still."

I do as he says, on the brink of disarray. A shutter sound, like a camera clicking, flutters through the room. He's documenting this.

"Perfect. You've been a very good girl. Are you ready for me to fuck you?"

"Yes." I pant, my skin inflamed, my body desperate, my pussy aching and soaking wet.

"Yes, what, baby?" Kayne massages my inner thigh.

"Yes, please fuck me. Make me come."

"Oh, I plan to." He spreads my folds wide and pours some wax right onto my swollen, throbbing clit.

"Holy shit!" My head spins and I buck in the swing as the burn of the wax does something inexplicable, makes my arousal magnify and my adrenaline spike almost like a runner's high.

"Shit. Please. Please, I need you," I beg as my climax teeters on a sharpened point.

"Say it again." Kayne rips the vibrator out of my pussy.

"I need you! I need you!" I chant.

"Again!" He slams into me, quelling the ache, feeding the flame.

"I need you!" I shout as our hips clash together over and over, until my muscles tighten and milk his erection for everything it's worth.

"Oh fuck, baby, come," he growls as I soak us both, my climax making a mess on his cock and my inner thighs.

"Fuck!" he hisses as he plows into my pussy, steady and hard, like he's cleaving through a turbulent sea. He doesn't stop thrusting until he's buried so deep, it feels like our orgasms become one.

"Kitten," he rumbles disoriented as he pumps in and out, emptying himself inside me.

Left slack in the swing, Kayne grabs my face and kisses me lethargically until we both come back around.

"How do you feel?" he asks between flicks of his tongue.

"Exceedingly used," I reply honestly, still unable to see him.

Kayne chuckles. "Exactly how you should feel. This is my

body and I'll use it however I see fit."

"You never disappoint in that aspect," I say, as he removes my blindfold.

"Did I hurt you?" He searches my eyes.

"Yes."

Kayne frowns. "You didn't use your safe word."

"I didn't want to use my safe word. You like hurting me and I like being hurt."

It's the ugly truth. I am the masochist to his sadist. I crave his pleasure at the same time demanding his pain. We are two misplaced pieces of a puzzle that fit perfectly together. And I wouldn't have it any other way.

Kayne unstraps me from the swing and helps me to stand. My wrists are sore from straining against the restraints, my pussy is tender from the rough fuck, and my skin is prickly from the hot wax.

"Take a shower with me?" I ask Kayne as I nuzzle up against his toned, naked body.

"Do you really need to ask?" He tilts my chin up.

"I wasn't sure if you wanted another one."

"If it's with you, I'd never say no. You should know that by now."

A smile is my only reply. In the bathroom, I inspect his masterpiece in the brighter light. The playroom was dim. I look closely at the way the wax runs along my body, the pattern almost looks like letters. Wait. It *is* letters. K-A-Y-N-E

"Are you serious?" I turn to him.

"What?" He grins, proudly.

"You wrote your name on my body in hot wax?"

He shrugs nonchalantly. "You're mine. Signed, sealed, and delivered."

Hmm . . . where have I heard that before?

All I can do is shake my head and laugh.

Crazy man.

ELLIE

I SPACE OUT AS MY mother chatters away on the other end of the phone. "Tara bought me this adorable pair of earrings. I loved them so much I made her get a pair for you. They're in the mail."

"Thanks, Mom," I half-heartedly respond.

"How's the weather?" She changes the subject for the fourth time, trying to engage me. "It's May and still cold here," she says frustrated.

"Sunny and eighty-five degrees," I inform her.

"I'm so jealous. I'm ready for some tropical climate. I keep trying to convince your father it's time to move."

I scoff to myself. "You know that man will never leave New York."

"I know." I can almost see her pout. "At least we get to visit soon. I can't wait to see you."

My parents make a trip out to Hawaii at least twice a year. I love it when they visit. My family is the one piece of my nearly perfect life that's missing.

"I can't wait to see you, too," I respond sullenly.

"Oh, honey. Try not to think about so much." Her voice softens. "It will happen when it's supposed to."

"If you say so."

"I do." She's resolute. "Dad wants to say hi. I love you."

"Love you too, Mom."

"How's my girl?" My father asks the same question in the same parental tone every time I speak to him.

"Fine, Dad."

"Mmm hmm. How's that husband of yours treating you?"

"Like a princess."

"He better be. Don't want to have to come out there and crack any skulls."

"Dad . . ." I actually chuckle. You know that old saying girls marry their fathers? I think it's true. A possessive, overprotective man raised me, and then I went and married one. Thankfully, as much as they are alike, my father and Kayne have a wonderful relationship.

"Miss you, sweetheart. I can't wait to see you."

"Me, too," I reply, trying to mask my blue mood.

I hang up with my parents and go back to staring at the picture on my computer screen. I've been looking at it most of the morning. A survivor and her five-year-old son standing on the Great Wall of China smiling brightly. It was accompanied by a thank-you letter I received in my inbox.

Dear Mrs. Stevens,

I can never say thank you enough for the generosity of your organization. I never dreamed I would leave the country, let alone get to experience another culture in such an unbelievable way. Hope and happiness are sometimes hard to come by, but you have given me both.

Sincerely,

Stacy

I usually love receiving letters like this. Hope and happiness, that's exactly what I want to provide. I receive so many requests, so many stories of pain and brutality, of people looking for an escape or distraction from their experiences, even if just temporarily. But seeing her hold her child in her arms does nothing but make me sad.

Kayne and I have been trying to conceive for over six months and nothing; not even a late period.

I inspect every feature of the little boy's face—shaggy brown hair, big blue eyes, and olive skin. But it's his smile that destroys me the most. He isn't looking at the camera; he's looking at his mother. Sometimes I wonder if I am being punished for not wanting to have children in the first place, and now that I do, more than anything, I feel like a failure as a woman. Like I'm incapable of doing the one thing a female is meant to do. Give her husband a child.

"Ellie?" I hear Kayne before I see him and discreetly wipe away the moisture in my eyes.

"Yeah?" I attempt to sound upbeat as he leans on the door-frame of my office.

"You ready to go?"

"I see you are." He's dressed in his black fatigues and gun holster, looking undeniably hot. My stomach flutters as I think back to the other night and how he arrested me for indecent exposure. What that man can do with handcuffs and a nightstick should be illegal.

I close my laptop and stand up, knowing I need either a cold shower or a firm fucking. Both of which will have to wait. Kayne is leaving on an overnight training exercise and dropping me off to stay with London while he and Jett are gone.

Grabbing my packed bag by the front door, I hop into our souped-up Jeep as Kayne locks up the house.

My mind wanders as we drive past all the beautifully manicured homes in the neighborhood. All pristine and vibrantly green.

"Are you and London going to behave tonight?" Kayne asks, squeezing my knee playfully.

"I can't promise anything. We get lonely when you and Jett are gone."

"I bet." He smiles salaciously, no doubt picturing us together.

"Still, you better behave."

"I don't think you have anything to worry about. I foresee a G-rated evening of nail painting, *Frozen,* and pizza."

Kayne shakes his head, his dark sunglasses concealing his eyes. "Poor Becks."

"He's a man, he'll sleep through most of it," I assure him.

Jett, London, and both children are outside on the expansive front lawn when we arrive. On cue, Layla darts across the grass to Kayne while London and Jett sit with a sleeping Beckett on a blanket.

"See, I told you." I nudge Kayne as we walk up. "Sleeping already."

He chuckles while throwing Layla around. "Higher, peanut butter!" she squeals, and Kayne obliges.

"What did you do?" I sit down next to London and grab a strand of her hair. She makes a face like she's not sure how she feels about the chop job.

"You like it?" she asks unsurely.

"I love it." Her long purplish red hair is now a shoulder-length bob.

"I feel like I needed to simplify my life."

"So you cut off all your hair?"

"It was a start. You'll understand when you have kids."

I drop my eyes. "If I ever I have kids," I mutter to myself.

London puts her hand over mine. It's her discreet understanding gesture.

"Okay! Time to go!" Jett stands up at a breakneck speed and snatches Layla right out of the air before she drops back into Kayne's hands.

"Daddy!" She giggles happily, and it tickles all of our hearts.

"Do you have to go?" She hugs him.

"It's only for one night," he assures her, their blond hair the exact same color in the sun. "And when I get back, we can go swimming in the ocean," Jett promises her.

"With swimmies," Layla says seriously. No messing around.

"Maybe without swimmies?" he tests the waters.

"Definitely swimmies. Mommy says I need swimmies until I can hold my breath under the water."

"You hold your breath under water when you're in the tub. Why can't you do it in the ocean?"

"There are no waves or fish in the tub!"

"Oh, is that the difference?"

"Yes!" Layla confirms, like *duh!*

"Okay then." He chuckles, placing Layla on the ground. "Be good for Mommy and Aunt Ellie."

"And be a good big sister to Beckett," she adds cheerfully.

"Yes," Jett agrees while kissing her little forehead. I dissolve.

London and I both stand up and say good-bye to our men.

Once out of ear shot, London purrs so only I can hear. "I hate it when they leave, but god I love to watch them walk away," she says as Kayne and Jett stride to the Jeep, muscled backs and tight asses on display.

I elbow her lightheartedly but can't dispute her claim; their butts do look great in those pants.

LONDON AND I BOTH COLLAPSE on the bed.

"Where do you and Jett find the energy to do anything else besides run after those kids?"

"The part-time nanny is our lifesaver. She'll be here bright and early tomorrow morning so I can actually sleep."

We had one crazy night keeping those children occupied, out of trouble, clean, and fed. Now that Beckett is running around, he never stops moving and gets into everything. I turned my back for one second and he had unraveled an entire roll of toilet paper into the toilet. Luckily, we caught him before he flushed. I left London to clean up the aftermath of that one.

"Are you sure you like my hair?" London asks self-consciously.

"Of course, I do." I twirl a strand around my finger. "You could shave your head and still look like a supermodel. I hate you for that."

"Stop." She taps me lightly. "I do not look like a supermodel."

"Sure." I close my eyes and smile. "Keep telling yourself that."

"Whatever." She brushes me off. "Wanna send a picture of us sleeping together to Kayne and Jett?"

I grin. "Yes."

London grabs her phone off the nightstand and shimmies up next to me.

"Okay, close your eyes." She positions the lens above us, rests her head on mine and then clicks away.

"Perfect." She picks out the best picture and then hits send with the caption:

London: Bedtime is no fun without you.

Her phone dings a few seconds later.

Jett: We'll bring the fun tomorrow night. Behave.

London: Behave? Now there's definitely no fun in that.

Jett: Send me a pic of your tits.

London and I both crack up. Men and their one-track minds. We pull our shirts up and send the boys more sinful selfies. Us kissing, touching, fingering, coming. That should hold all four of us over until tomorrow.

When we finally do go to sleep, I realize this has been the first night in a long while I haven't pined over what I don't have and appreciate what I do.

I WAKE UP WITH A sharp pain in my abdomen. "Oh." I roll over and try to breathe.

"London?" I shake her awake. "London."

"Mmm?"

"Ouch!"

"Ellie?" She opens her eyes.

"Something's happening."

"Something like what?" She sits up and throws the covers off us then gasps. "Ellie, did you get your period?"

"I just had it." I look down at the blood staining my inner thighs and the sheets. "Oh!" Another stabbing pain immobilizes me.

"Okay. Come on, up." She scoots out of bed. "We're going to the hospital."

"Hospital?"

"Yes." She rushes around her bedroom, putting on clothes

and pulling her hair into a low ponytail. "Go wash off. Where's your overnight bag?"

"Downstairs," I tell her as I slide carefully off the bed.

"I'll grab you a change a clothes and check on the kids. Then straight to the ER."

"Do you think that's necessary?" I ask and she creases her eyebrows.

"Absolutely. I'm not letting anything happen to you on my watch. Better safe than having to deal with the wrath of Kayne."

She has a point there.

"Okay." I walk slowly into the bathroom and turn on the shower. My stomach constantly tortured with cramps. As I wash away the blood, I worry what besides my period would make me feel this way. Vaginal cancer is the only thing that comes to mind. The thought terrifies me. My mother's sister was diagnosed at the ripe old age of thirty-five. The disease runs in my family. I dry off frantically and find my clothes on the stripped bed in London and Jett's room. Thankfully, the blood didn't stain the mattress. By the time I make it downstairs, London has the car keys in her hand and is kissing Layla and Beckett good-bye.

The ride to the hospital is tense and quiet. London holds my hand the whole way, while every bump jolts my fragile insides.

The ER is relatively quiet for a Saturday morning. Only one other person is in the waiting room.

"Please fill this out." The nurse behind the counter hands me a clipboard. I sit with London and fill out the paperwork in a fog.

"Do you want me to call Kayne?" London asks as I return to the clipboard to the receptionist.

"No." I curl into a ball next to her. "Let's just see what the doctor has to say." Although I'm pretty sure I might already know the answer. Maybe that's why I can't get pregnant? I'm sick.

"Ellie Stevens." A male nurse calls my name. London and I follow him through the door, past several pulled curtains, until we come to an empty alcove with a bed and strange machines. It reminds me of when I was in the hospital after I was shot. I shiver. I haven't been back to one in almost five years, and I was hoping the next time I did visit, it would be under happier circumstances.

"Okay." The young male nurse with light-brown hair and eyes looks over my information. "I see you've had some cramping and bleeding?"

"Yes."

"Any chance you could be pregnant?"

"No. I just had my period last week."

"Okay. And I see you have a family history of vaginal cancer."

I nod, close to bursting into tears.

"Well, I'm going to check your vitals, take some blood, and then the doctor will be in to see you."

I nod again, incapable of speaking.

"I'm John, by the way," he says kindly as he checks my pulse and takes my blood pressure.

"Nice to meet you," I reply softly, sinking into myself.

When he draws my blood, I wince and look away, concentrating on the small television in the upper left-hand corner of the room.

"All right." He picks up a tray with several vials of my blood. "I'll go get these to the lab and the doctor should be here shortly. It's not too busy this morning. For once." He smiles then walks off.

I once again curl up into a ball on the thin mattress and stare off into space. The cramps haven't subsided and there is a constant throbbing in my lower abdomen.

"How about some trashy TV?" London turns up the volume and scoots her chair closer to the bed. "I never got to watch television growing up. It was always piano lessons or French tutors or studying. It was such a sheltered existence," she reminisces.

She has told me this before, but it doesn't sound like she was sheltered; it sounds more like she's cultured and worldly.

"The only words I know in French are ménage à trois." I try to joke, but when I giggle, my sensitive muscles contract painfully.

"Those are really the only important ones," she jests.

London strokes my hair as I lay on my side miserably, watching trashy reality TV. I don't know how long we wait, but another episode of the same show comes on.

"Ellie Stevens?" An older man in a white coat announces my name.

"Yes, that me." I turn onto my back. He looks at me as if he recognizes me.

"I'm Doctor Holiday." He introduces himself as John rolls in a machine behind him. "We never formally met, but I'm the doctor who performed your surgery the night you were shot."

"Oh, yes. I remember hearing your name." I struggle to sit up.

"It's good to see you doing well." He smiles as he pulls up a chair next to me.

"I think that is yet to be determined."

Doctor Holiday grins slightly as he pulls up my shirt. "How's your fiancé?"

I look at him thrown. "He's my husband now. You know him?"

"We met briefly. Quite the intense individual."

London snickers. "That's one way to describe him."

Doctor Holiday pushes on my abdomen. "Any pain?"

"A little." I wince.

"Still bleeding?"

"No, I don't think so."

"Good." He takes a seat in the chair and plays with the knobs on the machine John rolled in. "When was the last time you had your period?"

"Last week."

"And everything seemed normal? Normal blood flow?"

I take a moment to think back. "Actually, it was lighter than usual, and it only lasted two days."

"Mmm hmm. A little warm." He squirts some jelly on my lower stomach. My heart starts to palpitate.

A few seconds later, a new nurse comes in with a folder. "Labs," she announces as she hands it to John.

"I think I already know what it's going to say." Doctor Holiday puts the wand of the machine against my belly and swirls it around. There's nothing at first, but then we hear it. A strange, underwater thumping sound.

"Oh, my god!" London slaps her hand over her mouth.

"Just as I suspected. John, can you confirm?"

John flips open the folder. "Yup. Positive."

"Positive for what?" I ask, behind the curve.

"Congratulations, Mrs. Stevens, you're pregnant. That's your baby's heartbeat you're hearing."

"What?" I repeat again in utter shock.

"Ellie, you're pregnant!" London erupts.

"But what about the bleeding? And my period?"

"That wasn't your period," Dr. Holiday explains. "You were spotting. It's normal, and the cramping is probably just from the implantation of the fertilized egg in the lining of your uterus. My advice is make an appointment with your OB as soon as possible and try to eliminate stress during your first trimester."

The information is a little slow to sink in.

"I'm really pregnant?"

"You heard it here first," the mild-mannered doctor beams.

"Can I hear it one more time? Just for a second?"

The doctor glances back and forth between John and London. "Sure. Why not."

"Give me my purse." I motion to London. She hands it to me and I pull out my phone.

"Okay."

Dr. Holiday puts the wand back on my stomach and the fast-paced underwater sound fills the tiny room once again, and I cry.

ELLIE

"HOW ARE YOU GOING TO tell Kayne?" London asks ecstatically as I wipe the jelly off my stomach and pull down my shirt.

"I have no idea." My voice is shaky from the shock. I'm not sure I even believe it yet.

I'm actually pregnant.

"I want another one," London abruptly discloses.

"Another one?"

"Yes, just one more."

"Think Jett will go for it?"

She nods. "I've always wanted a big family. He knows that. And maybe if we hurry we can be pregnant together."

"Oh, Jesus," I laugh loudly. "Could you imagine the hormones?"

"I can imagine holding two little ones at the same time." She's practically burning up with baby fever.

"You better be careful what you wish for. You might end up with twins."

London shrugs. "So be it."

"You're cra-" the chiming on the television catches my attention.

"WE INTERRUPT THIS PROGRAM WITH A SPECIAL REPORT," the newscaster announces. "EARLIER TODAY, OFFICIALS RECEIVED A TIP THAT TWO MISSING BOYS, JAMES ANTHONY AND RODNEY O'CONNELL, WERE BEING HELD IN A REMOTE HOME ON THE NORTH SIDE OF OAHU. THE TWO BOYS WERE REPORTED MISSING LAST THURSDAY AFTER NOT RETURNING HOME FROM A LATE SOCCER PRACTICE. THE OWNER OF THE HOME AND

SUSPECTED CAPTOR IS CHARLES TINLEY. TINLEY, A REGISTERED SEX OFFENDER, WAS THE PRIME SUSPECT IN THE DISAPPEARANCE OF THIRTEEN-YEAR-OLD JUSTIN COPELAND SEVERAL YEARS AGO, BUT NO CHARGES WERE EVER FILED. TINLEY ALSO HAS A HISTORY OF MENTAL ILLNESS AND HAS BEEN CALLED 'A THREAT TO HIMSELF AND TO OTHERS WHEN NOT TAKING HIS MEDICATION.'"

London turns up the volume as we listen more intently to the young, pretty newscaster speak. She's one of the anchors on the morning news show Kayne and I sometimes watch.

"EARLY THIS MORNING, A HIKER HEARD SCREAMING IN THE WOODS CLOSE TO HIS CAMPSITE. RICHARD PRICE FOLLOWED THE SOUNDS UNTIL HE CAME UPON TINLEY'S RESIDENCE. THERE, HE SAW TINLEY TORTURING ONE OF THE BOYS WITH A LIT CIGARETTE WHILE TIED TO A TREE. PRICE IMMEDIATELY CALLED AUTHORITIES. WHEN HE CONFRONTED TINLEY, TINLEY PULLED OUT A KNIFE AND RETREATED INTO THE HOUSE. PRICE MANAGED TO GET RODNEY O'CONNELL FREE, BUT WAS INFORMED THAT JAMES ANTHONY WAS STILL INSIDE THE RESIDENCE. ONCE OFFICIALS ARRIVED ON THE SCENE, TINLEY FIRED SEVERAL WARNING SHOTS AT THE OFFICERS WITH A SHOTGUN. WHEN OFFICIALS GAVE TINLEY THE OPTION TO SURRENDER, HE INFORMED THE OFFICERS HE WAS 'IN POSSESSION OF EXPLOSIVES AND WOULD BLOW HIM AND THE BOY UP IF THEY DIDN'T LEAVE.'

DUE TO THE NATURE AND SEVERITY OF THE SITUATION, HONOLULU SWAT WAS DISPATCHED AND HAS NOW TAKEN CONTROL OF THE SCENE."

That's when my stomach drops. The camera flashes to a live feed of the house, surrounded by a dozen and a half men dressed in black body armor. Some holding machine guns; some holding protective shields. The image is too far away to see any facial features, but both London and I know Kayne and Jett are somewhere in the mix of the Special Weapons and Tactics Team. All we can do is watch as the men carry out what they were trained to do—defuse violent situations. We sit in a frozen state as the team surrounds the tiny rundown house while too many antagonistic words play on repeat in my mind—*a history of mental illness, a threat to him and others, explosives.*

The men just hold their ground, while London and I hold our breath. What are they waiting for? I lived through the raid at Mansion, and Kayne had told me the story of my attempted extraction when Michael kidnapped me, but I have never really seen him in action, so to speak. Never witnessed firsthand how he puts his life on the line until now — *a history of mental illness, a threat to him and others, explosives.*

My lungs cycle oxygen sluggishly as the men descend on the house, kicking the door down and crashing through windows. But nothing prepares me for what happens next.

BOOM.

"It is reported several officers have sustained life-threatening injuries."

It feels like that sentence is stuck on repeat.

"It is reported several officers have sustained life-threatening injuries."

"It is reported several officers have sustained life-threatening injuries."

But they don't say which officers. We can't even see their faces as they're dragged from the wreckage. What remains of the house is nothing more than a pile of destroyed wood. It's been almost seventeen minutes since the bomb exploded.

"Charles Tinley is reported dead."

Is it wrong to be thankful of that and still be resentful because he hurt people in the process? Possibly hurt my husband or one of my best friends?

I feel sick. Like I want to throw up. Neither Kayne nor Jett are answering their cell phones, which only makes my rampant thoughts run wilder.

I compulsively twist my wedding ring around my finger. A white gold band with pink diamonds and the words, 'Ruined By Him' etched on the inside.

Kayne has a similar engraving on his, 'Owned By Her.'

He surprised me with the inscriptions during the ceremony.

I could barely hold it together as it was—then he showed me his little surprise, and it sent me right over the edge. That moment was perfect and beautiful and magical, and I know it can never be emulated again. Our wedding was a one-of-a-kind day; the same way my husband is a one-of-a-kind man. Anomalous. Unique. Irreplaceable.

The one person I could never live without.

"It is reported several officers have sustained life-threatening injuries."

The emergency room is in an uproar, no doubt preparing for the mass injuries about to barrel through the door. One of them possibly my husband. I clutch my stomach instinctively. This is supposed to be a happy day.

When the first gurney carrying a hurt officer rolls by my patient room, I lose the battle with my nausea and puke in the biohazard bag. My nerves just can't take this.

"Ellie." London holds my hair until the contents of my stomach are empty.

"I feel the same way," she tells me as I dry heave.

"Ugh. Yuck." I wipe my mouth.

"I know." She moves me back to the bed and digs around in her purse.

"Here." She pulls out a juice box.

I just stare at it. "Seriously?"

"Yes, seriously. I'm a mom. I come prepared. You'll be the same way, carrying around a bag of tricks." She rips off the little plastic straw, unwraps it, then stabs it in the hole.

"Thank you." I accept the purple and red box from her, take a sip, and swish the apple-flavored liquid around in an attempt to get rid of the nasty taste in my mouth.

That's when I hear a very distinct voice barking outside the little room. Both London and I barrel out of the alcove to find Kayne towering over my nurse, John. There's soot smeared on his face and dirt covering his clothes, but that seems to be the extent of his injuries. Unless you count self-induced hypertension. He's pissed.

"Kayne?" He glances over when he hears his name.

"Ellie?" I nearly knock him over when he looks directly at me.

"Where's Jett?" London asks frantically.

"In there." He tries to point to a room similar to mine, while I climb all over him.

"Baby, what are you doing here?"

I ignore his question. "Are you okay?" And instead ask my own. "I saw everything, the news report, the explosion . . ." My voice quivers. "They kept saying officers had life-threatening injuries but didn't say which ones."

My eyes tear as I cling to his shirt. If you think being married to a Dom is difficult, try being married to an ex black operative who is now part of an elite SWAT unit.

I would take the Dom any day.

"Shh, Ellie, I'm okay. Everything is okay." He runs his hand through my hair. That should soothe me, make me feel comforted, but it somehow has the opposite effect.

"You scared the shit out of me!" I lash out, slamming both fists on his chest. "I thought you were hurt!" I hit him again, crying. "Or worse!" The third time he grabs my wrists before impact.

"Whoa, killer. I'm fine. There's no need to beat me up," he says humorously, before his facial expression changes. "How did you know I would be here? Did someone call you?"

"No."

"London, then?"

"No. We were actually already here," I confess, sniffling.

"What?" His grasp tightens. "Why?"

Oh shit, this is not the way I envisioned telling Kayne he's going to be a daddy. Right after an explosion with a death grip around my wrists.

"I woke up bleeding this morning," I divulge.

"What? Where?" There's a mix of fear and anger in his eyes.

"Between my legs," I admit softly, so only he can hear.

"And you didn't think to call and tell me?"

"London rushed me to the hospital. I didn't want to worry you while you were away." Although, selfishly, in hindsight, I wish I had. That way he wouldn't have been anywhere near a crazy man with explosives.

"So what's wrong?" he asks concerned.

"Nothing," I tell him truthfully.

"Ellie," he says strictly. Like, *don't fuck around with me* strict.

"I'm pregnant." I rush the words out. They're amazing to say.

"What?" It looks like I just slapped him.

I nod. My angry tears turning into joyful ones.

"Honest to god?"

I nod more fervently, unable to speak from the overwhelming happiness.

"Holy shit!" He hauls me into his arms and plants an exaggerated kiss right on my lips. I wrap my legs around him and squeeze with every ounce of strength I have.

"But wait." He pulls away. "Why were you bleeding? Is something wrong?"

"No. The doctor says it's normal in the first trimester. I just have to keep my stress level low. Which has been a bit difficult this morning."

"I'm sorry. I didn't mean to scare you. I should have called and told you I was all right, except Jett got hit with some shrapnel and I needed to make sure he was okay."

"Is he?"

"As far as I know, it grazed under his eye. That part of the skin bleeds profusely. I think it looks worse than it is."

"Is that why you were yelling at the nurse? To get someone to check on him?"

"Of course."

"Were you inside the house when the bomb went off?" I ask meekly, unsure if I want to know the answer.

"No. Several of us had gone around back to extract the other boy. He was in bad shape. Beaten up, starved, and severely dehydrated. Once he was out, that's when the other team went in. Jett wasn't wearing his protective eyewear and caught some flying debris."

"Are the boys going to be okay?"

"I think so, but from what I understand, they were abused in more ways than one. We might want to send them a business card sometime down the line."

"Oh, no." I frown, a mash up of emotions hitting me.

"Tinley has a rap sheet a mile long, and most of it is child abuse."

"Disgusting monster."

"I couldn't have said it better myself."

"I'm just glad you're okay." I rest my head on his shoulder.

"I'm fine." He hugs me. "It's going to take more than a pipe bomb to get rid of me."

"I don't want to get rid of you. Ever."

"You say that now." He chuckles.

"I'll say that always." I close my eyes, suddenly exhausted. "Can we go home?

"Sure, kitten. We can take a nap right after you lick me clean." He nuzzles my neck.

I giggle. "Insatiable."

"It's who I am. *Love me or leave me.*"

"I choose *love you.*"

"I can only hope."

I roll my eyes, faithless man. "I need to grab my purse before we leave. Do you need to say good-bye to Jett?"

"Nah." Kayne starts walking in the direction London and I bombarded him from. "London is with him. I'll check in on him later."

I direct Kayne into the small space I spent most of the morning in. He sets me on the ground and I grab my bag.

"Wait." I stop him as he takes my hand to leave. "I didn't exactly tell you I was pregnant the way I wanted to. Or hoped to. Can we sit for a second?"

"Sure." Kayne looks confused but takes a seat on the bed anyway. I yank the curtain closed for privacy then crawl onto the mattress next to him. I pull out my phone and hand it to him.

"Am I supposed to call the baby?" he asks, even more perplexed.

"No." I laugh as I swipe the screen and hit an app. "Just press play."

He does, and a second later, that quickly pounding underwater sound pulsates through the air.

His eyebrows crease before understanding hits.

"Is that . . . ?" He brings the phone closer to his ear.

"The baby's heartbeat. I wanted you to hear it when I told you."

Kayne just sits there spellbound, listening to the rhythmic

sound. "It's the most amazing thing I have ever heard." His voice is breathy and his eyes are glassy.

I snuggle up against him. "I think so, too."

ELLIE

KAYNE STARES SILENTLY OUT THE living room window.

That's his position of choice these days. Leaning against the glass, ominously quiet, lost in his own head.

I'm six months today; my belly has finally popped and I have given up trying to squeeze into any of my pre-pregnancy pants. Maternity it is from here on out. I wish not fitting into my clothes was my biggest problem. Kayne had been over the moon about being a father up until about a month ago; when we went for my twenty-week ultrasound and found out we were having a boy. When, for the first time, we were able to see our baby's little feet and hands and face in a 3D picture. Everything changed after that. He retreated into himself. I know my husband, and beneath that cocky, *I'll break you in half* exterior is a high-strung, excitable man who needs to exercise restraint when it comes to his emotions. They can become a Molotov cocktail if he's not careful. Believe me, I know; I've been in the direct line of fire when he flies out of control.

Kayne walks a fine line every day, and lately that line seems to be getting narrower and narrower. It doesn't take a rocket scientist to know what he's thinking about. *Her,* his mother, his childhood, and all the shitty things that happened to him while growing up. I'm beginning to worry that starting a family is going to have a negative effect on him. That instead of completing us, it's going to tear us apart. I know I had reservations in the beginning, and I know I'll always worry, but what really scares me is the thought of raising this child alone.

"Hey." I speak to Kayne's back.

"What's up, kitten?" His reply is flat.

"I think we need to talk."

"Oh yeah, 'bout what?"

"What's bothering you."

"Nothing is bothering me," he fires back.

"We both know that's not true."

"I'm fine, Ellie."

"No, you're not. You barely sleep, you barely eat, and you haven't touched me in almost a month."

"Is that what this is about? You're horny?"

"No. That's not what this is about. It's about you and your issues."

"I have issues?"

"Lately, you do."

"The only issue I have is you accusing me of having issues." He's being obtuse and pissing me off.

"Kayne. In three months, we are bringing a child into this world. I want him to know his real father, not this watered-down version who can't even look at me."

"Are you saying I'm not the real father?"

I sigh exaggeratedly. "I'm saying you're an asshole who won't face what's bothering him."

Kayne finally turns around, anger burning in his eyes. Good. Finally, a reaction other than just aloof.

"Did you just call me an asshole?"

"I did. Do want me to repeat myself so you can hear it again?"

"That isn't a very nice thing to say."

"Well, I had to get your attention somehow."

"You have it. What do you want to talk about, Ellie?" His tone is menacing.

"What's bothering you."

"I told you, nothing is bothering me."

"I call bullshit. Your mother is bothering you. Your past is bothering you. Becoming a father is bothering you."

"Becoming a father isn't bothering me."

"But thoughts of your mother are?"

Kayne remains quiet.

"Maybe it's time you found out what happened to her," I suggest.

"Maybe not," he seethes. I know this is a gaping wound for Kayne, a painful buckshot right to the gut. But he has to face it and now is the time.

"I can't keep living like this. I need my husband back. I feel alone and scared and I don't want to do this by myself."

His expression softens but not enough to give me hope.

"I can't, Ellie."

"You have to," I push.

"I don't have to do anything," he argues.

"Yes, you do! For me! For our child!"

"Let me remind you of something, kitten," he snaps and I jump. "*I* own *you*, so that means *I* tell *you* what to do, not the other way around. And if I say no, it's no!"

"Kayne!"

"Enough!" he shouts at me. "Go find a corner to curl up in and leave me alone!"

"You condescending cocksucker!" I hiss. Outraged, I pick up the remote control off the coffee table and hurl it at him as hard as I can, missing his head by a half inch. It smashes into the window behind him, creating a starburst crack.

"What the fuck, Ellie!"

"I'll do better than find a corner. I'll find a new placc to live!" I storm out of the living room crying, snatch my keys off the kitchen counter, and slam the front door behind me.

I DROVE AROUND FOR HOURS, knowing without fail I would end up here.

I ring the doorbell and London answers moments later.

"Hey." She hugs me.

"Expecting me?"

She nods. "Kayne was here a little while ago looking for you. He said you had an argument."

"Argument is an understatement. I cracked one of the windows in the living room."

"One of the big ones?" Her eyes widen.

"Yup," I confirm.

"Did you try and put his head through it?"

I laugh. It feels cathartic. "I threw the remote at him and missed. Let's hope this baby doesn't inherit my accuracy." I put my hands on my protruding stomach. "Is Jett around? I need to talk to him."

"Upstairs. He just finished giving Becks a bath. Somehow, he got into the pantry, climbed on the shelf, and opened the peanut butter jar. The kicker, instead of eating it, he decided to rub it all over his body and the kitchen walls."

"No." I gasp.

"Yes." She sighs exasperated.

"And you want another one?"

"If I change my mind, it's too late now."

I stare at her funny. "Are you . . . ?"

London nods precariously.

"Oh!" I hug her. "You're insane and a little bit my hero."

"Mommy?" Becks calls for London from the top of the stairs.

"Here, baby." He walks down all clean. Blond hair blow-dried and blue eyes mischievous.

London lifts him into her arms. "Mommy has a baby in her belly," he tells me in his sweet little raspy voice.

"I heard." I smile at the gorgeous little boy.

"And let's hope he or she only looks like you." London touches her forehead to his. Becks chortles spiritedly, like he understands his mother's joke. "Go on upstairs, Ellie. I need to give this little rascal some dinner."

"Okay." I walk up the stairs while London carries Becks into the kitchen. I love London and Jett's house. It is so warm and full of love with pictures of them and the children everywhere. My favorites are the artistic shots in black and white. London loves photography and is extremely talented with a camera. I've already recruited her to take the baby's first newborn shots.

Upstairs, I find Jett rinsing out the tub.

"A father's work is never done," I quip as I lean against the doorframe.

"Nope. And I wouldn't have it any other way." He flashes a smile at me, the front of his shirt soaking wet.

"I hear congratulations are in order, *again*," I say cheerfully.

He grins brightly, confirming the news. "Yes, they are."

"You're going to have a baseball team by the time London is done with you."

"If that's what she wants." He dries his hands off and comes to stand in front of me. "How are you doing, sweet thing?"

"I want to kill my husband," I reply half-serious, half-sardonically. "You have some peanut butter . . ." I point to his hair.

"Yeah, we've all been there." He rakes his fingers through the front of his blond strands, removing the clump of peanut butter. "Little bugger," he muses.

"Who? Kayne or Beckett?"

"Both," he shoots back.

I can't stop myself from laughing.

Jett washes off his hands, tickled. He is the most laid-back father. Nothing seems to rattle him, even Becks' most outlandish antics. When he's finished drying them, he puts his arm around me and walks me down the hall to his office. "Let's talk."

I take a seat on the cozy loveseat across from his desk. He always jokes he bought the piece of furniture for his therapy sessions. Right now, it's coming in handy.

"I heard Kayne was here," I say.

"Yup. Looking for his lost kitten."

"Not lost, runaway. There's a difference."

"Yes, there is," Jett agrees. "What was the fight about? Had to be pretty bad if you left."

I groan. I'm irritable, frustrated, and utterly exhausted. "He's been distant. Barely talks or eats or sleeps."

"How long has this been going on?"

"About a month. Ever since we went for my twenty-week exam."

"I see," Jett ponders.

"When I finally confronted him today, everything just blew up." I make an explosion gesture with my hands.

"He was pretty upset you left. Probably has half the SWAT team out looking for you right now."

"Good, let them look. Serves him right for dismissing me

into a corner like I really am a naughty cat."

"He didn't." Jett's eyes widen.

"Oh, he did. That's when I threw the remote at him and stormed out."

"Did you hit him?" Jett asks overly interested.

I shake my head.

"Too bad. I would have loved to see your throwing arm." He chuckles.

"It's not as impressive as you may think."

"So what do you think his issue is?"

"The same issue that has been bothering him his whole life."

"His mom." Jett provides the obvious answer.

I nod, sadly. "I just think he needs to face it. And he won't listen to me. He just pushes me away. I know the baby is affecting him. He was so excited to be a father, and now, he's just completely different. He's shutting us out, and it's terrifying me."

"Ellie, listen." Jett takes a seat on the couch and wraps one arm around me. "First, I want to be clear. Kayne will never abandon you. And if the thought even crosses his mind, I'll kill him, and I'll make sure it hurts. Second, you'll never be alone. No matter what happens, you have me and London and we love you like family."

"Thank you." I rest my head on his shoulder. "That's very reassuring, but I'm not worried about me. I want our child to know his father. Know the person I know. I really think you need to talk to him. Convince him that he needs to find out what happened and put the past to rest. It's the only way he's going to move on."

Jett stiffens before he lets out a huge sigh. "Ellie, I think there's something I need to tell you, and I think now is definitely the time."

I look up at him warily. "What?"

Jett gets up from the couch and walks around his desk. He opens a drawer, pulls out a folder, and drops it on the desktop.

"What's that?"

"The smoking gun."

"Huh?"

"It's a copy of Kayne's caseworker's file. The one who was assigned to him when his mother was trying to regain custody."

"What?!" I fly to my feet.

"How long have you had this?" I snatch the folder up and open it. The contents contain a bunch of papers and a picture of a seven-year-old Kayne sad enough to break your heart into a million pieces.

"Since right before we went undercover together."

"What." You could knock me over with a feather right now. "That's like . . ." if my math is right, "over ten years."

Jett confirms with a reluctant nod. "I had to be prepared in case of any surprises. So I looked into what happened to her."

"And . . . ? What happened?" I flip through the file looking for answers. "Where is she?"

Jett's expression just gets bleaker. "She's dead, Ellie. She died shortly after Kayne met her for the first time."

"No." My chest tightens.

"I'm sorry."

"How?"

"A car accident."

"No, I mean how does Kayne not know this? He was in the system. He had a caseworker. Wasn't it their responsibility to tell him?" I ask irate.

"I have a theory about that."

"A theory?" I huff.

"Yes. At the same time Kayne's mom was working to gain back custody from the state, Kayne was living with two of the most abhorrent foster parents in Motor City. It doesn't say this in the file, but I believe what happened was when the social worker showed up unannounced to deliver the news, she caught the couple abusing Kayne. It says she 'found him locked in a small broom closet, dirty and naked and smelling like urine.'"

"Oh, god." My stomach turns. Animals.

"I believe, since it doesn't say much after that account, the social worker didn't want to traumatize Kayne further. So when she removed him from the home, she didn't tell him about his mother."

"Okay, well, she should have told him eventually, no?"

"Yes, I'm sure, but researching further, I came across the elderly woman's death certificate. In an unforeseen twist of fate, she apparently died of a heart attack three days after she removed Kayne from the household."

"You're shitting me."

"I could not make this stuff up."

"So your theory?"

"She never got a chance to tell Kayne that his mother didn't up and abandon him, and his next caseworker was unaware he didn't know or didn't bother to tell him. Either way, the information slipped through the cracks."

"That's almost too impossible to believe."

"Crazier things have happened. A woman once gave the man who kidnapped her, lied to her, and forced her to submit a second chance, and now she's having his baby."

I squint petulantly at Jett. We are not talking about me and my questionable decisions.

"We need to tell him. We need to just bite the bullet, tell him, and hope we survive the wrath of Kayne." I pace the room.

"Hold that thought." Jett pulls his phone out from his back pocket and glances at the screen. "That wrath may come sooner than you think," he informs me before he answers it. "Hey, man. Yeah," he looks directly at me, "she's here."

Oh, shit.

"Okay . . . see you in a few." He hangs up. "You're done blowing in the wind."

"Apparently. You just gave me up."

"We have like seven seconds before he gets here."

"Should we take cover?"

The doorbell rings.

Too late.

"At least he's using his manners and didn't break down the door," Jett points out.

"He probably just doesn't want to pay for another home re-pair."

"Ellie!" Kayne's voice blasts through the house.

"Up here!" Jett yells back.

Moments later, Kayne appears in the doorway. He's wearing loose jeans and a fitted blue t-shirt. His hair is a mess — my guess from trying to pull it out — and there's a hollow look in his eyes.

"Let's go." He tries to grab my arm, but I step back.

"No." I see the devastation on his face, but we have to do

this. We have to address the albatross in Kayne's life.

"Ellie, now." His tone becomes stricter, desperate almost.

"We need to talk." I hold my ground.

"No, we don't."

"Yes. We do." I'm adamant.

"Maybe you should listen to her," Jett interjects.

"Maybe you should mind your own fucking business. She's *my* wife—"

"Yes, I know," Jett cuts him off sharply. "You love to remind everyone of that. Maybe you should remind yourself why you married her. Wait. I'll do it for you. Because she has your best interests at heart and only wants what's best for you. *For you* and *your* child."

Kayne immediately clams up. I know he wants to argue with Jett, wants to tell him to fuck off and drag me out of the house, but he's exercising his restraint. He may be excitable, but he's not stupid.

"Sit." I gesture with my head to the couch. "Jett has something he needs to tell you."

"I'd rather stand."

"For fuck's sake! Can you not be difficult for one minute today!?" I erupt and the baby kicks me. "Oh!" I double over.

"Ellie?" Kayne grabs me. "Are you okay?"

"Yes, I'm fine, but you're pissing the baby off. Now can you please just sit?" I grimace. "I think he has your front kick." I rub my sore stomach.

"Fine," Kayne grumbles, dragging me to the couch with him. "But if I sit, you sit."

"Fine," I spit back. Such a loving couple, aren't we?

"What do you have to tell me?" He directs his question at Jett, tension emanating from his pores. He may be trying to play it cool, but he is a bundle of nerves.

Jett takes a deep breath and leans on the edge of the desk directly across from us. With compassionate eyes, the eyes that are the most genuine on the planet, he recites almost verbatim what he told me only minutes ago. About Kayne's mother, the social worker, and his 'theory.' Kayne remains silent the whole time . . . barely blinking, barely breathing. Once Jett finishes, you could hear a pin drop.

Kayne is intimidating to begin with, but menacingly-silent Kayne is downright scary.

"Kayne." I lace my fingers with his and rub my thumb across the back of his hand. He doesn't utter a word, not one, single word. After a few moments, he spontaneously stands up, hauling me with him with a death grip on my hand. He stalks over to Jett, who straightens, pushing out his chest, almost defensively. Kayne glowers as he reaches for the folder, never breaking eye contact with Jett. The tension in the room could suffocate a tyrannosaurus rex. Once he has it, he drags me away, quieter than a mime. Outside the house, he opens the door to his Jag and motions for me to get in.

"Can you drive right now?" I ask as he walks around the front end.

No answer. He just slips into the front seat and hands me the folder. He punches the ignition and takes off in the direction of our home. Peeling through the quiet neighborhood, we make it there in record time.

"Kayne." I try to engage him, but he shuts me out, not even acknowledging my attempt. After we're inside, he drags me upstairs to our bedroom. Taking the folder from my hand, he drops it on the dresser then proceeds to strip me of all my clothes. Every single article until I'm completely naked and he is still fully dressed.

"Lay down," he orders, his tone downright daunting. Guardedly, I crawl onto the mattress and rest my head on the pillow. Kayne kicks off his shoes then follows right behind me. To say I'm not a little apprehensive would be a lie. I don't think my husband would ever intentionally hurt me, but when his emotions become too much for him to handle, he tends to get rough. And with me being pregnant, I'm not sure how that will fair.

Kayne slides his hand over my naked body, feeling every microscopic inch of my skin, before he lies down next to me. Practically wrapping me up like a mummy with his limbs, he places his head on my bare chest and begins to cry. Hard, deep sobs that shake us both. I'm completely thrown, but at the same time, completely sympathetic and a little destroyed. He finally knows the truth and now has to deal with it.

"Shhh . . ." I kiss his head and run my fingers through his hair, encouraging him to purge all the feelings out.

"*Shhh . . .*"

I WAKE UP ALONE AND to the smell of breakfast. My stomach growls. Someone is hungry.

I slide out of bed, grab a cotton sundress from my closet to slip on, brush my teeth, and use the bathroom. Once downstairs, I find Kayne working away in front of the stove. Whatever he's making smells delicious. I walk quietly up behind him, not to scare him, but because I'm not sure what frame of mind he's in. Yesterday, he confronted his darkest demons; who knows how that's affecting him today.

"Hey," I say softly as I stand next to him.

"Morning." He kisses me on the head while he continues beating — "Eggs? You're making eggs?" Now that I'm close, I see a host of different ingredients spread out on the counter — pancake batter, butter, milk, chopped green peppers, and shredded cheddar cheese. I also notice his caseworker's file laying open off to the side. I have no doubt that he's been reading it. If I know him, dissecting it would be a better word. "You hate eggs. They remind you —"

"Not today," he cuts me off. "Today, I love eggs. Today is a new day." He scoops up the chopped peppers with his hands and drops them into the bowl then pours the half cup of shredded cheddar in afterward.

I feel like I'm in the twilight zone. "*Today, I love eggs. Today is a new day.*" *What?* For the past five years, just looking at a carton of eggs made Kayne shudder because it reminded him of Kim, the foster mother who tried to seduce him when he was seventeen. Making eggs was apparently their "thing".

"How long have you been up?" I glance at the clock. It's only seven forty-five in the morning.

"A while. I couldn't sleep, so I worked out. We need a new

punching bag, by the way. Then I went for a run with Jett around six. I showered, and now here I am." He dumps the eggs into the heated frying pan and they sizzle.

"And how are you doing?" I ask delicately.

He pulls in a deep breath and then exhales, pushing the eggs around with a wooden spoon. "I think I'm okay."

"You're *okay?* Some serious information was dropped in your lap yesterday and you're *okay?*"

I don't mean to sound skeptical, but this is my husband we're talking about. Usually, he reacts quite passionately when railroaded with information.

"Ellie," he huffs, putting down the spoon and turning to face me. "I have spent damn near my entire life obsessing. Wondering what, why, how. I don't want to do it anymore. I'm finally going to take Jett's advice and just put the past behind me. I have more important things to worry about now." He puts his hand on my stomach. It's such a sweet gesture, I almost tear up. Damn hormones.

"I have one memory of my mother, and it's a happy one. She wanted me, and that's what I'm going to remember."

"Really?"

"Yes."

Okay, I won't lie. I'm flabbergasted. I didn't expect this when I woke up. I thought I was going to be putting him back together one tiny piece at a time, but it seems Kayne had some revelations while I was sleeping.

"You're the most important thing in my life. I'm sorry if I've disappointed you lately." He kisses the inside of my wrist.

"You didn't disappoint me. You scared me."

"I know." He pulls me closer and drops his forehead to mine then kisses me again before stirring the eggs around. "And I'm sorry for being a condescending cocksucker."

"It's okay. You can't help who you are," I tease him.

Kayne smirks. "Brat."

"And proud of it." I grab a little piece of green pepper and pop it into my mouth.

"Clearly." He snakes his arm around my waist and secures me against him. "You're the only one who can tame me, Ellie."

"I'm not interested in taming you." I run the tip of my nose up his neck. "I like you just the way you are."

Kayne tightens his hold, his eyes flashing with excitement. I quiver.

"Are you hungry?" he purrs.

"Starved." My mouth waters for more than just eggs.

"I bet."

My stomach interrupts us, growling loudly, and we both laugh. "Someone is impatient."

"You missed dinner last night. Can't blame him."

"He eats just like you."

"If that's the case, let's go feed our boy." Kayne sucks and licks my lips before he lets me go.

I grab some plates and silverware, while Kayne finishes cooking the eggs and pulls out a stack of pancakes warming in the oven. Once everything is set up on the patio outside, we sit down to eat. Well, Kayne sits. I kneel between his legs, but not as a submissive, instead just a woman who is madly in love with her man.

"My mother's name was Sarah," Kayne proceeds to tell me as I take pieces of pancake from his fingers. "Sarah Rivers. She had me when she was fourteen. There was no mention of my father on my birth certificate." I chew slowly, listening attentively. "She was hooked on drugs and in no condition to raise a child, so the state took me away from her when I was thirteen months old. She eventually got clean and pulled her life together. She was twenty-one when she died." I run my hands over his thighs as he speaks. "She wanted me."

"Of course she did." My composure nearly shatters. "She was your mother. Of course she wanted you." I take his face in my hands and kiss him. A deep, emotive kiss that screams I want him, too.

"When we have another baby—"

"Another one? We haven't even had this one." I laugh.

"Well, when, if, we have another baby, and it's a girl, I want to name her Sarah."

"That's fine. Done deal," I agree immediately.

"Good." It's almost like he sighs with relief. Did he think I would say no to such a heartfelt request like that? He then attacks my mouth, smothering it with passion-fueled kisses.

"Aren't you hungry?" I ask when we break for air.

"Starved. But I want dessert first."

It doesn't take long before our hands are roaming all over each other and breakfast is a distant memory. I guess I wasn't the only one starving in more than one way.

"Touch me, Ellie." My name vibrates low and deep in his throat as I pull on the waistband of his basketball shorts and jerk his rock-hard cock with both hands. He kisses me more aggressively, his fingers tangled securely in my hair. After a few pulsating seconds, Kayne lifts me to my feet and pushes me back so I am leaning against the edge of the table. Forcefully, he spreads my thighs then buries his head between my legs. I hold on to the table for dear life as he licks through my folds incessantly, my knees nearly giving way.

"*Ohhhh* . . ." I moan insufferably as the sweet ache of pleasure spreads through my whole body. "Yes," I pant rapidly as my climax electrifies.

"Oh no," Kayne removes his mouth from my ravished pussy. "Not this time." He pulls down his shorts just low enough so his cock pops free. "This time, you're coming all over me." He hauls me up into his arms and impales me onto his straining length. My muscles immediately tighten, shocking my arousal.

"Oh, shit," I mutter helplessly as Kayne hooks his arms under my thighs.

"Already, baby?" He impales me onto his thick rigid cock over and over, like he's doing bicep curls with my body. Drawing me all the way up then dropping me all the way back down.

"I can't help it," I wince as he slices through me, my muscles painfully contracting and my clit tingling. "It's the hormones, all you have to do is look at me and I pop. *Oh, god!*" I practically screech when I come, my control crumbling to pieces.

Kayne growls against my neck as he fucks out every last drop of my orgasm, demanding my demise like he always does. I barely have the strength to hold onto his neck as he walks us inside and lays me down on the dining room table.

"This is exactly how I want you." He thrusts deeply into my depleted body, pushing up my dress. "Destroyed, shattered, ruined, demolished."

I moan incapacitated, exactly all those things and more. He

ravages me repeatedly, plundering my pussy with no apologies, taking exactly what belongs to him. My pleasure.

"I love you like this, Ellie." He places both hands on my stomach and slows his pace. "I love that a piece of me is inside you." He caresses my little bump.

"I love it, too," I respond in a state of ecstasy.

"Come with me, kitten?" Kayne rubs my clit and I arch my back.

"Yes, please. Please make me come." He knows just how to touch me; he knows all my secret spots.

"Hurry." He rubs harder, circling his hips, punching his swelling cock into my dripping wet channel.

"Don't stop." I exhale sharply as another orgasm forms like a cyclone. "Kayne! Kayne!" All I can do is cry his name as he calls forth my arousal, my addiction. The sensations that bind me to him.

"Kitten." He slams into me once, twice, three severe times, right before we fuse as one.

"Fuck, Ellie." Kayne stills as I shudder around him, stretched and filled to the point of breaking.

Lost in our own little post-coital world, my husband worships me with his mouth like he loves to do, covering my entire body with lingering kisses. My favorite — the one he plants right in the center of my stomach.

"That's how it's done," I hear him whisper.

"Kayne!" I scold him, teasingly.

"What?" Gotta teach him early." He laughs.

I am only capable of responding with an eye roll.

Men.

ELLIE

"THIS KID NEEDS TO COME out, now!" I complain miserably, sprawled out on the bed. The baby is a week late and showing no signs of wanting to grace the world with his presence.

"He's comfortable in there. He knows how good it is." Kayne makes an off-color joke.

I smack him with a pillow. "Well, Mommy is ready to have her body back." I'm hot, swollen, and convinced my bladder has disappeared with how much I pee.

"We can go for another walk?" Kayne suggests.

"No. If I walk around the block one more time, I may scream."

"Have sex?"

"Definitely not."

"Thai for dinner? Maybe some spicy food will light a fire under him."

"No."

"Just want to lay here and be miserable?"

"Yes," I whine.

"Can I go work out while you're parked on the bed?"

"Abandoning me when the going gets tough already?"

It's Kayne's turn to hit me with a pillow.

"I'd never abandon you."

"I know. Sure, go ahead." I sigh. "I'll be here . . . fat, miserable, and immobile."

"Miserable?"

"Miserable."

"I promise I'll bring you up some ice cream when I'm done." He gets up off the bed.

"I won't get too excited. Your workouts are like four hours long."

"I'll make this one fast." He chuckles and leans down to kiss me.

"Oh!" I sit up suddenly and end up colliding with Kayne's face.

"Ouch, Ellie you just head-butted me," he rubs his nose.

"I'm sorry. I got a pain." I stroke my huge stomach.

"Are you okay?" He sits back down on the bed then immediately shoots up. "Did you pee?"

"What? No! Oh shit! I think my water just broke!"

Kayne looks at me stunned. "He heard you."

"Good! At least I know he listens." I push myself up and swing my legs over the side of the mattress. This is gross. "We have to go."

"Ya, think? Good thing I'm trained for emergency situations." He helps me stand.

"You are not delivering this baby in the backseat of our car."

"If we don't get you to the hospital soon, I might."

"Shit!" I nearly keel over as another contraction hits.

"Quick, we gotta change your clothes and get out of here."

"I need to take a shower first."

"What?"

"I'm all sticky. I need to shower."

"Ellie, we don't have time."

"It will only take a second. I can't show up at the hospital with amniotic fluid dripping down my thighs. Just please get me something to wear while I wash off."

Kayne grumbles. "You better not be cursing me when I tell you to push in the backseat of the Jeep."

"You're not delivering this baby in the car! Now go!" I waddle into the bathroom and hop in the shower.

"I'll remind you of that when you have your legs spread wide open and dangling over the roll bar!" he yells over the shower.

If he were close, I would punch him. This kid makes me very aggressive.

I clean up in record time and change into the shorts and T-shirt Kayne grabbed for me.

"Ready?" Kayne has both of our hospital bags slung over each shoulder.

"What about the bed?" I ask. "We should clean it up."

"It's going. I'll order a new mattress and have it express delivered."

I won't argue with that.

As I walk down the stairs, another contraction hits. "Oh!" The pain shoots up and around my stomach and lands right in my lower back.

"Ellie? Are you okay?"' Kayne holds me up by my arm. I swear I could just sit right here and never get up.

"I'm not sure." I breathe heavily in and out.

"Come on, we have to go. Now."

My contractions come on hard and fast, and by the time we get to the hospital, Kayne is clocking them at three minutes apart.

I can tell you, the maternity ward is no-nonsense and efficient. The minute we got here, I was put in a delivery room, hooked up to a fetal monitor, and examined thoroughly.

"Do I have time for an epidural?" I ask the nurse after she checks my cervix.

"Unfortunately, no. You're at eight centimeters with contractions less than three minutes apart. This baby is coming soon."

"Shit. Shit!" Another contraction begins, making me see stars. The pain is in my back and utterly excruciating.

"Fuck, this hurts." I crush Kayne's hand. "I don't know if I can do this without drugs."

"Ellie, you have to. You heard the nurse. He's coming soon." There are so many emotions in my husband's voice.

"I can't."

"You can, just breathe. You're strong enough."

"You're going to have to keep reminding me of that."

"Till death do us part, you know that."

I can only nod frantically as another contraction pummels me.

"They're getting closer." Kayne looks at his watch while he holds my hand. There is ungodly pressure between my legs, like

I'm about to rip in two. I almost hate him for being so calm.

The nurse comes in to check on my progress again. "How's Mom doing?"

"Dying," I whine.

"Ellie," Kayne snaps at me. "Not even funny when it's a joke."

"I'm not joking!" I scream as another wave of pain hits.

"Hopefully, it will be over soon." She measures my cervix again. "Oh!" Her face perks up. "It looks like we need to page the doctor. You're fully dilated." She smiles, removing her latex gloves. "As soon as he gets here, you can start pushing. Hang on for a few more minutes."

That seems like an unbearable amount of time.

The pain is constant now, just a steady stream of agony.

"Ellie." My doctor walks into the room smiling brightly. I'm glad someone is in a good mood.

The OB practice I go to has several doctors, all of whom I met and could potentially deliver the baby depending who was on the floor. Luckily, my main doctor is at the hospital today.

"So, looks like we're ready." He pulls up a chair and sits right in front of my wide-open legs. I have been told childbirth is beautiful and wondrous, but up until now, I've felt more like a lab rat, poked and prodded with my lady bits on display than an excited mother-to-be.

"Okay, Ellie. We're going to push," Dr. Hanini tells me. "On three."

"Okay."

"One. Two. Three." I push with all my might, hoping the baby comes out on the first try.

"Good. Relax." Dr. Hanini is in his late forties, has golden brown skin, and is native to Hawaii. I connected with him the minute he walked into the room. He just has this wonderful calm energy and the nicest bedside manner. Even Kayne likes him, which is saying a lot since he's seen my vagina just as much as my husband has over the last nine months.

"Again, Ellie." I push once more, squeezing Kayne's hand for dear life.

"Come on, baby, you can do this." Kayne is peering down over my legs to see what's going on.

"Can you see anything yet?" I ask, drained already.

"Nothing, not yet," he tells me.

"Gotta keep pushing," the doctor encourages me.

And I do, for over two excruciating hours.

"WHY WON'T HE COME OUT!" I'm crying by this point, exhausted and ready to pass out.

"A little more, Ellie. You need to hold on a little more," Dr. Hanini urges me to keep going.

"I can't. I'm so tired," I protest, nearly delirious.

"Ellie, come on. Strong enough, remember?" Kayne wipes some sweat away from my brow and feeds me some ice chips. "You've been through worse than this."

"Okay," I pant, determined to push this kid out.

With a deep breath, I summon the little bit of energy I have left and push again. It feels like something gives way and suddenly there is a little less pressure.

"Good, Ellie. His head is out!" Dr. Hanini exclaims, and then his expression turns grim. "Stop. Stop pushing."

"What? I can't stop!" Now that the baby has momentum it feels like I no longer have control. My body is on autopilot.

"Fetal heart rate is dropping."

"What?" I look back and forth between Kayne and the doctor. Both their faces are expressionless, but Kayne's eyes are wild.

"What's happening? What's going on?"

"Ellie, try to relax. The cord is wrapped around the baby's neck," one of the nurses informs me in a palliative tone.

"One second." Dr. Hanini works quickly, doing something I can't see.

"Please hurry! I have to push!"

"Okay, now!" The doctor gives me the green light. I barely even push before I see a still, silent, little blue infant being lifted into the air. I nearly pass out.

"Let me see him! I need to see him!" He's not crying and all the nurses are crowded around the doctor and my baby.

"Kayne!" I grab his wrist, but he's still as stone as he watches the hospital staff work on our child.

My emotions spin further out of control every second there's no sound.

I don't know how long time lingers before we hear it.

The first wail of our newborn son.

It breaks me out of my petrified state of panic.

"Is he okay? Please tell me he's okay."

"He's perfect." One of the nurses places him on my chest, and I burst out into tears.

"We just needed to suction him."

I hold him close as he squirms, instantly bonding with the helpless little angel. I fall in love for the second time in my life. I look up at Kayne. He's stiller than a glassy lake. I think he's in shock. Actually, I know he is.

"Say hi to your son."

Only his blue eyes move. From me to the baby and back again.

Definitely in shock.

"Okay. Time to clean up this little fella." One of the nurses lifts him off of me.

"Already! I just got him."

"It will only be for a few minutes, and then I'll give him right back." She's a sweet woman, very smiley, but I still give him up reluctantly.

Kayne tails the nurse, putting his super stalking skills to good use and hovering already.

"What's his name, Mom?" One of the other nurses in the room asks.

"Alec. Alec Jett Stevens. AJ for short." I wipe away my happy tears as they fall one by one.

"Jett? Oh, I like that." She smiles coyly.

If you knew him, you'd like it even more.

Kayne and I both wanted to name him after someone important in our lives. Who's more important than my father and Jett?

I watch as Kayne's towering figure spies on everything the nurses do to AJ, while at the same time battling with fatigue.

The adrenaline that was keeping me awake is now fading fast, exhaustion settling in its place.

"I HAVE SEEN A LOT of nasty shit, oops, I mean stuff. Daddy needs to learn to watch his language, but that black tar in your diaper takes the cake." I hear Kayne before I even open my eyes.

When I crack them open, I watch silently as he wraps AJ up in a little blue blanket and lifts him from the hospital's bassinet.

"I know you've only been here a few hours, but I think now is a good time to have our first talk."

Kayne sits down in the rocking chair in the corner of the room and proceeds to talk to the tiny bundle nestled in his arms. AJ looks even smaller when he holds him, like an oversized peanut.

"First, and this is extremely important, always keep your head down and hands up in a fight." He lifts one of AJ's little hands to his face. It doesn't surprise me in the least that that's the first piece of advice he shares with his son.

"Second, ketchup is delicious on eggs. Don't let anyone tell you different. Especially Mommy.

Third, don't be afraid to talk to girls. Uncle Jett may need to help you with this in the future. Daddy isn't very good at it. It's the only thing Daddy isn't good at." The arrogance is blatant in his voice. Heaven help me.

"Lastly, and this is the most important, it takes courage to love. Mommy taught me that. She's the strongest, most resilient person I know. She was brave enough to love me, and it changed my entire life. So try to be a good boy for her. I already give her enough grief." Kayne's tone gets softer as he kisses AJ's forehead. He's so sweet with him I could melt.

"When did you learn to swaddle?" I ask, interrupting the love fest.

Kayne looks up at me and smiles the most brilliant smile I have ever seen.

"While you were sleeping. The little man and I were having some quality father-son time."

"And how is that going for the two of you?" As if I didn't already know.

"Amazing." Kayne glances down lovingly at AJ. "How do you feel?"

"Better." I sigh. "I want to see him."

Kayne walks AJ over to me. He handles him like a natural. When I take my first good look at his little face, my heart nearly explodes with joy. His eyes are open and alert, and he's trying to fit his entire fist into his mouth. I think someone's hungry.

"He's so perfect, Ellie," Kayne breathes.

"He is," I agree.

Ten tiny fingers and toes, a little mouth shaped like a heart, and vibrant blue eyes just like his daddy.

Kayne sits down on the edge of the bed, reluctant to give AJ up. "For nine months, I felt like a spectator, and now that he's here and I can actually hold him, it all suddenly feels real." Kayne draws his gaze away from the infant. "How did this happen?" he asks in awe. "How did this become my life?"

I laugh softly. "Evolution?"

"No." He shakes his head resolutely. "A miracle."

"Knock knock," a soft voice rasps just before Jett, Layla, Beckett and a very pregnant London walk into the room. She's having a girl, and they're naming her Shia.

Kayne turns his head, and clears the emotion from his throat before he faces our extended family.

"I want to see!" Layla rushes to Kayne, and stands on her tippy toes. He leans in slightly to show the children AJ.

"Baby." Beckett giggles trying to touch him.

"There's going to be one of these in your house soon," Kayne tells him.

"They can't wait," London informs us, putting a loving hand on Becks' blond head. He returns a little chicklet-toothed smile.

Kayne hands me AJ and steps back so Jett and London can get a better look. I cannot put into words what it feels like to hold my child. It's surreal. A manifestation of two people who's more beautiful and more perfect than I ever dared to imagine.

London caresses AJ's sweet little cheek with the tip of her

finger. "I love him already, Ellie."

"I do, too," I reply, brimming with emotions I never knew I had.

Kayne and Jett just look on like two proud lions protective of their pride.

"You've done good, grasshopper." Jett elbows Kayne.

Kayne clenches his jaw and flares his nostrils. *"Please* don't make me kill you. I don't want to shed blood on such a happy day."

Jett laughs melodramatically. "Like *you* could ever kill *me.*"

London and I just roll our eyes in response to our husbands' ceaseless banter.

No matter how crazy or life-altering the moment, some things will just never change. . . .

KAYNE

C.S. LEWIS ONCE SAID, "LIFE is too deep for words, so don't try to describe it, just live it."

That quote simplifies my whole existence. It reminds me to let the past be the past, let the present be the present, and let the future be the future. For a man who loves control, I've learned sometimes you just have to let go. I'm not afraid to do that anymore, because I know if I fall (which I do a lot) there is always someone there to catch me. And she catches me every single time.

I watch Ellie playing with AJ in the backyard from the kitchen. He wants her to pick him up, but she's doing everything in her power to keep him on the ground. She's eight months pregnant with our second child, and I know she's exhausted. AJ demands most of her attention. The two-and-a-half-year-old is as aggressive as his father and as loving as his mother. He's the perfect split, right down to his looks. My face with Ellie's green eyes and light-brown hair.

"Okay, time for some juice and a rest." She carries AJ into the house.

"Dwink! Dwink!" he demands.

"Bossy little thing," Ellie comments as she grabs a juice box from the refrigerator and then sits AJ on the countertop next to me. "Wonder where you get that from?" she jokes with him, and he smiles from her playful tone.

I smile, too. What can I say? Like father, like son.

"How's my girl?" I put my arm around Ellie as AJ sucks down his apple juice.

"Busy." She grabs my hand and puts it on her stomach so I can feel the flutters. "She always knows when you're close. She's a daddy's girl already. I'm going to get replaced pretty soon."

"No one could ever replace you." I lift her chin with one finger. "When I asked how my girl was, I meant you."

"Oh, well, in that case, I feel fat, bloated, and completely unattractive."

"Nonsense. I see sexy, alluring, and completely gorgeous."

"Daddy needs his eyes examined," she says flippantly to AJ, once again causing him to giggle.

As much as she complains about being fat and tired and pregnant, to me she really is the sexiest thing in the world. No amount of chains or collars or restraints can compare to the way she looks in a sundress with a baby growing in her belly.

Being a father changed me profoundly. I always thought I saw Ellie, but I didn't. Not really, not the way I see her now. I'm completely consumed with love—love for her, love for our children, and love for this life I was miraculously blessed with. Love that envelops me, sustains me, and grounds me. Before Ellie, I thought I knew my fate—a faceless man living a life undercover, just drifting along. But that's the funny thing about life. You never know what direction it's going to shove you in. I never thought I would fall in love, never dreamed of getting married or having a family, yet here I am with an amazing wife, a beautiful son, and a daughter on the way. I don't think words can express the depth of my happiness. The monumental gratitude I feel every time I look at my family. *My* family. The idea was such a foreign concept, but now that I have everything I never knew I wanted, I would do anything to keep us together. Keep my children safe and my wife happy. *Anything.* I killed for Ellie once; I wouldn't hesitate to do it again.

"Cupcake!" AJ squeals. "Mommy, pwease! Pwease! Cupcake!" He points to the miniature, chocolate frosted cupcakes sitting on the counter.

"Okay, just one." Ellie picks him up and places him in his

high chair.

"Sugar before sleep? Always works for me," I tease her.

"Good because you'll be the one putting him down."

"Oh?" I laugh at her as she peels off the wrapper and hands AJ his fudgy treat.

"Yup." She licks some frosting off her finger.

As I watch my son devour his snack, I can't help but think how one simple lick of a cupcake tilted my world on its axis and spun it in a completely different direction. Yes, life definitely is too deep to be described, it can only be lived.

"Kayne, what are you thinking about?" Ellie asks intuitively.

I possessively slip my arm around her waist and pull her against me. "Just how much I love cupcakes."

The End

ACKNOWLEDGEMENTS

IF YOU ENJOYED RUINED, AND the unplanned extension of Kayne and Ellie's story, you can thank my beta readers. After a lengthy discussion after finishing Claimed (I'll spare you the details) Ruined came to be. I will tell you I was pleasantly surprised they wanted (if I am being honest, demanded) more of their story. So I wrote it. For them, and you, the loyal readers who love Kayne and Ellie as much as I do. Thank you for spending your precious time with the Decadence family and taking a chance on me.

As with my other books, Ruined could not be what it is without help from some amazing people. I am really so lucky.

My editors, Candice Royer — thank you for being as neurotic about spelling and grammar as I am — and Jenny Sims, who always reminds me to 'clean up'. My beta readers, Jaime, Heather, Alecia, Jennifer, Amy, Debbie and Sarah who provide me invaluable feedback. Sarah, nice catch by the way!!

To Jaime Burns, my PA, and Linda Russell, my PR, who both work tirelessly to get my books in front of readers. You ladies are quickly becoming my solid foundation! My proofreader, Nichole Strauss and formatter, Christine Borgford from Perfectly Publishable, thank you for making the inside of my stories as pretty as the out. You ladies totally spoil me and I know it!! My cover designer, Marisa Shor, from Cover Me, Darling, thank you for pulling out a triple cover reveal in three days!! You, too, spoil me. To Give Me Books, for coordinating my cover reveals, giveaways and blog tours. Working with you is effortless. Thank you for that!!! To all the blogs who have supported me along the way! Without your help and rabid love for these characters, I don't know where I'd be! You are instrumental to an author's success! To my Instagram peeps! @NAbookaddict @73jem @romantic-bookbabe and @readingwhore. You have made Instagram my favorite social media site to play on! Always, to the survivors of sexual abuse and human trafficking. I write these books with you in mind and always donate a portion of my sales to organizations who help combat human trafficking. #FindPeace

Lastly, to my husband, who never signed up to go on this crazy journey with me, but is gladly taking the ride. Without you my life would be chaos. I am yours, signed, sealed and delivered.

PLAYLIST

Angels ~ The xx

Animals ~ Maroon 5

Sex and Candy ~ Maroon 5

Heartbeat Song ~ Kelly Clarkson

Lights Go Out ~ Fozzy

ABOUT THE AUTHOR

M. NEVER RESIDES IN NEW York City. When she's not re-searching ways to tie up her characters in compromising posi-tions, you can usually find her at the gym kicking the crap out of a punching bag, or eating at some new trendy restaurant.

She has a dependence on sushi and a fetish for boots. Fall is her favorite season.

She is surrounded by family and friends she wouldn't trade for the world and is a little in love with her readers. The more the merrier. So make sure to say hi!

Visit my Website: *www.mneverauthor.com*

Or find me on:

Goodreads
Facebook
Instagram
Twitter
Pinterest

BOOKS BY

 NEVER

DECADENCE AFTER DARK

Owned

Claimed

Ruined

Printed in Great Britain
by Amazon

63101764R00064